Also by
and ... Evans

Maggie Malone and the Mostly Magical Boots

Maggie Malone Gets the Royal Treatment

Maggie Malone

Makes a Splash

Jenna McCarthy and
Carolyn Evans

sourcebooks
jabberwocky

Published by Sourcebooks Jabberwocky, an imprint of Sourcebooks, Inc.
P.O. Box 4410, Naperville, Illinois 60567-4410
(630) 961-3900
Fax: (630) 961-2168
www.sourcebooks.com

Library of Congress Cataloging-in-Publication Data is on file with the publisher.

Source of Production: Versa Press, East Peoria, Illinois, USA
Date of Production: March 2015
Run Number: 5003534

Printed and bound in the United States of America.
VP 10 9 8 7 6 5 4 3 2 1

We dedicate this book to Bindi Irwin, whose work with her late dad, wildlife expert Steve Irwin, inspired the character of Marina Tide.

Table of Contents

Dear Maggie,

I know you're wondering why I sent you some dirty, old cowboy boots for your birthday. Your dad will tell you it's because I'm crazy, but the truth is they were mine when I was your age. I've carried them around the world with me twice, just waiting for your twelfth birthday. They might look like a boring pair of boots to you, but trust me when I tell you things aren't always what they seem. These boots will change your life, Maggie. If you let them, that is...

Love,
Auntie Fi

Chapter 1

When I Realize I Need to Find My Thing

Fridays are my second favorite day of the week for obvious reasons, but today started out even better than most.

For one thing, I woke up having a killer hair day without even trying—which, with my crazy head of curls, happens about as often as I win the lottery. Then my mom made me pumpkin pancakes *and* bacon for breakfast. Of course, I ate them together sandwich-style, even though my BFF Stella says that's the most disgusting combination in the entire food universe.

I've tried arguing with her—hello? What about Cheerios and clam sauce? Banana pudding and onions? Chocolate chip cookies and gravy? But Stella can be as stubborn as any mule you ever met, and she insists she'd pick any of those over my dream-team breakfast. Someday I may have to make her a hot-fudge-and-fish-sticks sundae. I'll bet she comes around.

The third awesome thing about today is we're having a huge pep rally first thing. It's supposed to get us all pumped up about this weekend's big basketball game against Washington Middle School, but I'm excited because I hear the pep rallies at Pinkerton (my new school since my dad lost his job) last, like, three hours, and that means I get to miss social studies. Don't get me wrong; normally it's one of my favorite classes. But the teacher, Mrs. Grossbottom, throws a "surprise" pop quiz every Friday (which makes it not much of a surprise, but it's not like anybody is going to point that out). I'm definitely not bummed to be missing out on *that* action.

I cruise on my bike into the Pinkerton parking lot, and the first thing I notice is a huge group of boys wearing suits. I'm talking about business suits, like my dad used to wear every day, with ties and everything. *That's weird*, I'm thinking when I notice a different group of guys and girls wearing bathrobes. *Even weirder! What is this, dress-crazy day?* I'm locking up my bike when Alicia pulls up next to me.

Alicia is my PBF (Pinkerton best friend). It's not that she's not as cool as my BFF Stella, but I haven't known Alicia very long. Besides, you can only have one BFF and Stella scored that title a million years ago. Anyway, Alicia is funny and cool and practically the mayor of Pinkerton. Usually she's a stylish dresser, but today she's wearing soccer shorts and a Pinkerton Pit Bull jersey. Yeah, our school mascot is a dog that's not known to be the friendliest breed around. Don't get me started.

"You ready to rally?" Alicia squeals, slinging her backpack onto her shoulder and holding up her hand for a high five.

"What's with the outfits?" I ask, giving her hand a hearty smack. My palm stings after I do it, but I firmly believe if you're going to do something, no matter what it is, you should give it your all.

"Oh my gosh, didn't I tell you?" Alicia asks, looking worried. "On pep rally days everyone wears their team uniforms! Oh Maggie, I feel terrible! I can't believe I didn't think of it."

"It's okay," I tell her. "I'm not on a team anyway."

"But Maggie, you *have* to be on a team! Otherwise

3

where will you sit at pep rallies? The teams all sit together. Plus, being on a team is really fun. Hey, are you any good at soccer? We could use a few more strong players!"

"I'm positively awful at soccer," I admit as we make our way through clusters of cheerleaders and flocks of feather-headed marching-band kids.

"Bummer," Alicia says.

"What's with the bathrobes?" I whisper.

"Swim team," she explains.

"And the suits?" I ask.

"Debate team," Alicia says. "You'd be good at that!"

"I don't really like arguing," I tell her. "Besides, I hate having things tight around my neck. I'd suffocate in a tie."

"The girls don't have to wear ties," she says, laughing. "They wear these cute little scarf thingies."

"I just don't think I'm debate team material," I say, shaking my head.

"Fair enough," Alicia agrees. I give her a weak smile. "Don't worry," she adds. "You'll find something." I look around and don't see a single kid not wearing some sort of team getup. A marching band guy next to me bends down, and his feather pokes me right in the nose.

"It looks like I'm going to have to find something," I tell her.

We're gathered with everyone else outside the Pit Bull Arena, which is the name for the school gymnasium. The energy in the crowd is intense and people are getting pretty impatient. I'm starting to worry there's going to be a stampede or something when I spot Mr. Mooney, the principal, waving his arms at the front of the throng.

"Can I please have your attention?" he shouts. Nobody stops talking or even pays him one lick of attention, so the office secretary, Mrs. Dunst, hands him a giant megaphone. I cover my ears.

"Can I please have your attention?" Mr. Mooney bellows into the thing, and this time you could hear an ant hiccup.

"Thank you very much," he continues, his words echoing off into space. "Everyone, please line up with your teammates and I'll call you in alphabetical order. We'll start with the band and then the baseball team."

Everyone starts milling around and forming into

matching groups, and I have no idea what to do. Does every single kid at this school belong to a team? And what if you belong to two or three, say soccer and yearbook and chess club? I guess you go with the one that comes first in the alphabet. Or maybe the one with the coolest uniform.

I feel a tug on my arm. It's Elizabeth, the other new-ish girl who moved to Pinkerton the same week I did.

"Are you on a team?" she whispers. Elizabeth is a super-quiet talker, so a lot of the time I only get about every third word. But today I know exactly what she's saying because I was about to ask her the same thing.

"Nope," I say. "You?"

She shakes her head sadly.

"What do we do?" she asks. "Where do we sit?"

"I don't know," I tell her. "I guess we go in last."

We stand there looking—and feeling—totally lost. The computer club is called and then the cross-country team. Elizabeth and I watch helplessly as group after group is admitted to the arena: Lacrosse. Math team. Quilt club. Spanish. Volleyball. Wrestling. Yearbook. Finally the only ones left are the teachers and me and

Elizabeth, and maybe a dozen other kids. We shuffle into the gym and make our way to the only seats left: nosebleed section, far corner. I settle in next to Mrs. Shankshaw, my million-year-old biology teacher.

"Tums?" she says, reaching into her sweater pocket and offering up a lint-covered roll.

"Oh, I'm good. Thanks," I lie. My stomach is actually a mess—but I don't think it's anything a dusty Tums will fix.

Chapter 2

When I Decide to Take the Plunge

I ride my bike home from school thinking about how weird it is that I have to join something at this new school just to *be* somebody. I mean, not to brag or anything, but I can be anybody I want whenever I want. I've already been a famous rock star and a for-real princess in England. I could wake up and be an astronaut tomorrow if I felt like it! I bet if they knew that over at Pinkerton Middle School they'd be singing a different tune.

It may sound ridiculous, but it's true. For my twelfth birthday, my crazy Auntie Fi sent me something that looked totally lame but turned out to be better than all the double-dipped doughnuts in the world: a pair of Mostly Magical Boots. They're called MMBs for short. They look like boring, old hand-me-down cowboy boots, but when I put them on and say the magic words, I get to be anybody in the world for an entire day.

Sure, they came with some rules, like I have to do something good during my borrowed day...and I can't tell anybody about the MMBs or the magic will disappear right off them... Oh yeah, and I'm not supposed to jump into them just to avoid something stinky that's happening in my real life. Which brings me back to my current dilemma: I need a team to join, like, lickety-split!

When I get home, I head straight for my desk and start making a list of possible activities. I'm not the cheerleader type. Chess makes my brain feel swimmy, and serving a volleyball hurts the inside of my wrist so much it makes me squeal like a stepped-on puppy. It's kind of embarrassing. I'm really good at math, but I'm not about to become a mathlete and spend my weekends competing in pre-algebra TriMathlons all over the state. (I'm pretty sure my parents wouldn't be too into that either.) When Stella brought me to her soccer team's "bring a friend to play" day, I *did* score a goal. Unfortunately, it was for the other team.

I'm scrolling through the extracurricular activity list on the Pinkerton website when Stella busts into my room and scares the daylights out of me. I think technically that expression means you faint, and I didn't actually go lights-out. But almost. I've got to hide that hide-a-key in a new place.

"Wassssup, Mags?" Stella says, flinging her backpack into the corner next to mine and flopping onto my bed.

Before I can catch my breath and answer, she says, "Willis Freedman is a total turd. You should be so glad you don't have to deal with him anymore."

Stella and I are totally opposite looking on the outside, but a lot the same on the inside, which my mom always says is the only part that really matters. Stella has shiny, pitch-black hair that's stick straight. I, on the other hand, was blessed with mounds of crazy strawberry-blond curls and a milky white complexion. Did I mention Stella has a tan even in the winter? It's so not fair.

Neither is the fact that I don't get to see Stella nearly as much as I used to since I had to leave Sacred Heart and switch to Randolph J. Pinkerton. I've made some good friends, but it still feels like something is missing. Maybe it's because Pinkerton is so big, or maybe it's because I'm still pretty new there. My dad says I just need to give it more time, and he's probably right. Besides, I don't really have a choice in the matter. If you ask me, that's probably the most unfair part of it all.

"What did Willis the turd do this time?" I ask, sprawling on the bed next to her. By the way, Stella has had a crush on that turd since the second grade. Oh, she totally denies it, and even though she Willis-bashes every chance she gets, anybody with two eyeballs can see she gets all loud and giggly whenever Willis is in earshot. That's a dead giveaway, if you ask me.

"Oh, you'll love this," Stella says, sitting up. "In French class, Mrs. Bernard made Willis a team captain so he got to choose three people for his Tour de France team, which is so stupid, but anyway. He was all, 'Sssssammy Strickland, Sssssarah Munson, and Sssssss…' He was looking at me the whole time—you know I'm the only other *S* in the class. He must've dragged that letter out for a full minute before he finally said, 'Leonard Kurtz.' I came *this close* to jumping on him like a spider monkey."

"Except that you wouldn't do that 'cause you heart him!" I say, jumping off the bed before Stella can pounce on me.

"Do not!" she protests. "Just because I gave him my leftover Valentine's candy two years ago does *not* mean I like him! The box only had those gross chocolate-covered cherries left in it!"

"Whatever you say," I say, letting it go because that's an argument I'm never going to win with Stella.

"Whatcha looking at?" Stella says, peering over my shoulder and happy to change the subject.

"I think I need to be more extracurricular," I tell Stella. "Everybody at Pinkerton is on some sort of team, so I'm trying to figure out something fun to do."

"Softball's fun," Stella suggests, grabbing a *Tween Scene* magazine off my desk and flipping it open.

I give her *the eyebrow*. "Have you forgotten about the famous Fourth Grade Concussion Incident?"

"Oh, right. Sorry," Stella says. "Student council?"

"Already elected for the year," I tell her. She nods and keeps flipping pages.

"Wait, does Stink—sorry, Pinkerton—have a swim team?" Stella asks. "You're a great swimmer!

Remember last year when you held your breath longer than Ginger Poole *and* Madison Greenway at Ginger's end-of-summer party? Man, she was so mad!"

"I do remember that," I tell Stella. "And you're right. I *am* a pretty good swimmer. Remember at Itchy Bitey I got a ribbon for being the only camper who could swim to the farthest buoy underwater without coming up for air?" The camp is actually called Camp Ichemytee after some famous springs that were discovered by Native American settlers. But mosquitoes are a major problem at Camp Ichemytee, so everyone calls it Itchy Bitey. It just fits.

"And," Stella shouts, "remember how we won first place in the synchronized swimming competition with our routine, the one where you stood on my shoulders at the end and did the giant jazz-hands belly flop? We were amazing, weren't we?"

"We really were," I agree, remembering the pink belly burn I got from my award-winning belly flop. That thing lasted for hours, but it was totally worth it.

"And get this," Stella says. "My cousin is on the swim team at her school in Florida, and they got to meet Marina Tide and even touch Skipper! That's a pretty sweet perk. In five years all my soccer team has ever gotten to do was tour the sock factory downtown. I only went thinking maybe I'd score some cool free socks, but they didn't give us squat. Talk about lame."

"Who's Marina Tide?" I ask, way more interested in somebody with a cool name like that than a sock-factory field trip. Stella looks at me like my neck just grew another head.

"Okay, please don't tell me you really don't know who Marina Tide is. Her dad is Flynn Tide, that famous guy we watched that show about during Shark Week?"

"The oceanographer?" I ask. "I remember now. But I didn't know he had some super-cool kid."

"Well, he does, and she goes all over the world saving stuff in the ocean and has her own pet dolphin, Skipper, who swims along next to their boat. I watched about a hundred MeTube videos of her the week I was out sick with strep throat. I can't believe I never told you about it!"

Stella boots me out of my computer chair and pulls up a web page with Marina Tide front and center. She's in the middle of the ocean with her long, blond

15

hair slicked back with water, and she's smiling like her face is about to split open. And it's easy to see why: She's got her arms around a dolphin like he's an over-sized Labrador retriever with fins for legs. The caption says "Marina Tide and her best friend Skipper."

"'Famous deep-sea explorer Flynn 'the Fin' Tide has devoted his entire life to ocean conservation," Stella reads. "'With his daughter, thirteen-year-old Marina Tide, Flynn travels the world on his ninety-foot trawler, the *Sea Angel*...' A trawler is a kind of private airplane, by the way." Stella nods her head so confidently that I feel bad correcting her.

"Actually, it's a boat," I say. "My Grandpa Winston used to have one. But it wasn't ninety feet long! That's bigger than my entire house. I could *totally* live on a boat that size. I only puked once on that Disney cruise we took two years ago, and I'm pretty sure that was because of the nasty shrimp cocktail my mom made me try."

I shudder just thinking about the Pink Puke Fiasco.

Stella clicks back to the Pinkerton website.

"Pinkerton *does* have a swim team," she shouts. "You should join!"

I think about this for a minute. I do love to swim. My favorite is being underwater and just floating there like a big *X*. It's like you're part of the water and totally by yourself and nobody can bother you. Only that's not true because last summer, as I was enjoying that free-floating feeling at the community pool, I got yanked out around the neck by an overeager lifeguard. Happy free-floating feeling? Over.

"I don't know," I tell Stella. "I mean, I'm a great swimmer and all, but I'm not sure my technique is all that good."

"That's what practices are for! Hey, look. Team tryouts are this Monday afternoon at the Mountain View community pool," she squeals, pointing to the big red circle on the online calendar. "Are you going to do it, Mags? You should totally do it!"

"Why not?" I tell her. "Maybe if I get really good, I can travel the world and swim with dolphins and save some big important coral reef."

"Saving a reef is probably seriously good karma," Stella says with a laugh.

My Auntie Fi taught me and Stella all about karma. You know, what goes around, comes around?

Like, if you sneak into your sister's room and search and search until you find her diary and then read it from cover to cover, you shouldn't be surprised if you wake up the next morning with a pimple the size of a grapefruit on your chin. That just means you stirred up some bad karma. It happened to Stella once.

"I might need some extra-good karma to make the team," I tell Stella nervously, eyeing the Pinkerton Minnows team photo. "Look at the shoulders on *her*," I say, pointing to a girl who looks like she could beat my dad in an arm-wrestling match.

"Well, if this little squirt made it, I'm thinking you're not going to have a problem," Stella says, pointing out a tiny girl in the front. The photo is sort of fuzzy, so I squint to get a better look at her. She's half the size of most of the other swimmers and has a big, bright, friendly smile. She's probably somebody's little sister that they let squeeze into the picture because she's so darned cute and sweet. That's my theory, anyway.

Turns out, my theory is about as far off the starting block as you can possibly get.

Chapter 3

When I Belly Flop Before I Even Hit the Water

"Well, I think that pep rally on Friday made it pretty obvious," I tell Elizabeth as we're being shuffled through the lunch line. "Oh, no thank you…" *Squish, slop, drip.* I try to pull my tray from the lady with the ladle but she's holding her side with a kung-fu grip. "I'm sorry. I wanted my rice *without* gravy, please." The lady with the ladle ignores me so I take my tray.

"Made what pretty obvious?" Elizabeth whispers.

"That we have to pick something. Anything. We can't hang out here in no-man's-land much longer," I explain.

"Oh, uh, okay…I guess you're right," Elizabeth stammers, picking up an apple and placing it on her tray.

She's really very agreeable, which is something I kind of love about her.

"I think I'm going to join the swim team," I announce, wedging myself between a guy from the chess club and a boy basketball player. Elizabeth does the same across the table. "You should do it with me!"

"Oh...I...I don't know," she says timidly, opening her carton of milk. "I'm not that great of a swimmer."

"Who cares? That doesn't matter!" I say, leaning across the table. "I mean, okay, I won't lie to you. I'm pretty good. Better than pretty good, I guess." I picture myself accepting my first-place ribbon at Camp Itchy Bitey. That really was awesome. "But that's not the point! It's just about being on the team—no matter how good you are."

"Maybe you're right," Elizabeth agrees, stabbing a Tater Tot with her fork. "I'll give it a shot."

"Then it's settled. Tryouts are this afternoon at Mountain View Pool. We can go together!" I explain, spreading a see-through napkin across my lap. I know there's really no point to a napkin like this, but I try to maintain high standards of good manners— even at RJPMS. "And I'm wearing this super-cute ruffled tankini my mom got me on sale at the end of the summer."

"That sounds perfect. I've just got a plain, old navy one-piece," Elizabeth says, looking a little disappointed.

"Again!" I say, encouraging her. "It doesn't matter how good you are, and it doesn't matter what you wear. It's just about being on the team!"

After school we swing by my house and then Elizabeth's to get our gear and head over to Mountain View Pool together.

"This hill is a killer, don't you think?" I ask Elizabeth, huffing and puffing and finally getting off to walk my bike.

"We moved here from Denver so the hills don't really get me too bad," she says, pedaling effortlessly up the steep grade.

"Too bad Pinkerton doesn't have a cycling team!" I yell as she passes me like I'm standing still.

Elizabeth waits for me by the door to the gym while I lock up my bike. Once inside, we see a bunch of parents and kids yelling and elbowing their way toward a folding table in the middle of the foyer.

A pair of large double doors slams hard against each other.

"I need everybody, and I mean *everybody*, to take ten steps back and form a civilized line," booms a voice moving to the other side of the table. Pretty intense for a swim team called the Minnows. Aren't minnows, like, the tiniest, most harmless, most sure to be eaten by other fish in the sea—or the lake, or the river, or wherever it is they live? As everyone scrambles to form a line, I see the body that's attached to that big voice. It's a man, more like a giant, probably seven feet tall. Okay, maybe not that tall, but the dude is massive, with broad shoulders and the longest arms I've ever seen. Last year in school, we learned about the great albatross, a bird that has a wingspan of more than eleven feet. Fingertip to fingertip, I bet this guy's is about the same.

"That's Coach King," Elizabeth whispers, sliding into place next to me. "I hear he's a little scary."

"I think you heard right," I whisper back. "And why is everyone so worked up? It's just a silly swim team." That would have been fine, no big deal, if the whole crowd didn't shut up right at the moment I said, "silly swim team." A sea of heads whirl around and stare me down. I feel like a gazelle about to be pounced on by a bunch of hyenas in one of those too-scary-for-normal-TV nature shows. Elizabeth takes a tiny step away from me, and I can't blame her. I look past the line of kids and parents (why didn't I ask my mom to come with me to this?) to see Coach folding his extra-long arms and peering around the crowd at me.

"And what's your name, miss?" he asks. I can't tell if he's fuming or not, which makes me even more nervous.

"Oh! Me?" I answer back, tightly clutching the bedazzled tote I made at art camp last summer and making my way to the front of the line. "I'm Maggie. Maggie Malone. That's Maggie with two *G*s, and Malone is spelled just like 'alone' except there's the *M* in front so it's not really all alone. Get it?" I say with a grin, but I get nothing. *Tough crowd.* And this is not good because when there's an awkward silence, I feel an uncontrollable need to fill it with words. "Technically, I'm Margaret Flannery Malone, if you need that for your files. My friends call me Maggie. My family is Irish—Scotch-Irish, actually, and my

Granny Malone? She came over on the boat way, way back—"

"Got it," Coach stops me before I have a chance to take him through the Flannery side of the family tree.

"You can go back to the end of the line now, Margaret," he says, making notes on his clipboard.

Well, that was kind of awful. The worst part is, I have no idea how much more awful things are about to get.

Chapter 4

When I Make a Splash (and Not in a Good Way)

It takes me forever to stuff my crazy head of hair into my swim cap, and it's still sticking out in about thirteen places. But if there was an award for cutest swimsuit, I'd totally win it. We're lined up waiting for instructions by a white tile wall that surrounds the indoor pool, and I scope out the competition. Everyone else is wearing boring old one-pieces so my hot-pink and neon-yellow ruffled tankini really stands out. I try not to act like I realize I'm the only one here with a sense of style.

"Cute suit," says a tiny voice from behind me. I turn around and smile. It's the adorable little girl from the swim-team photo!

"Aw, thanks," I say. I want to say something nice

about her suit too, but it's this old, faded gray thing and I just can't lie. It's a curse sometimes, honestly. "I like your goggles," I say instead, which is a pretty silly thing to say since there's really nothing special about them. But I like them better than the suit, so at least it's true. She gives me a toothy smile.

"What's your name?" I ask her.

"Brianna King," she says shyly.

"I'm Maggie Malone," I reply. "My real name is Margaret, but everyone calls me—" Coach interrupts me with his big booming voice.

"Jenkins, King, Malone, O'Connor, on your blocks!" he shouts. Elizabeth and I swap nervous glances. Elizabeth's last name is O'Connor, which when you say it all together makes it sound like her name is *Elizabetho Connor*, but who cares about that right now? I'm just glad that her name puts her on the starting block next to me. I feel a little bad when tiny Brianna steps up onto the block on my other side. I mean, I really want to make the team but I don't want to crush her like a bug or anything. I smile at Brianna but she just adjusts her goggles and looks right past me. She must be so nervous she can't even *see* me.

"Swimmers, on your mark," Coach calls. I notice that Brianna drops to a crouch position and puts her hands by her feet. The poor thing looks like she's trying not to fall into the pool! I hope she doesn't. That would be *so* embarrassing for her.

"Get set," Coach shouts, and since I have a great sense of rhythm and I know *go* comes next, I time my plunge perfectly. I nearly lose my bottoms when I hit the water, but I hike them up quickly and I'm pretty sure nobody saw anything. Well, maybe a tiny sliver, but definitely not a full moon. I coast clear down to the bottom of the pool. I just love it down there. It's so peaceful and quiet. I pull through that water, giving it everything I've got. *Man, am I flying! I'm like an underwater eagle slicing through this water! Or a submarine wearing a jet pack! I'm a mermaid, a graceful, nimble water nymph!*

I start to wonder why I didn't go out for the swim team at Sacred Heart, or even the community All-Star team. After all, I'm practically a fish! A sailfish, to be exact. We learned in biology that those are one of the fastest fish in the ocean. They can swim up to eighty miles per hour! I'll bet I'm going at least half that fast right now—and I'm just getting warmed up! I wonder if I'll win a medal this year, or maybe even a trophy.

I've never won a trophy in my whole life, if you don't count that baby gymnastics class Stella and I took when we were in preschool. "Everyone's a winner!" was the Tumbling Tots slogan, and if you stuck it out for the whole twelve-week session, you got a junky plastic trophy. Mine broke in the car on the way home from the last class. Anyway, I'll bet if I got a real one for actually winning something, my mom would get me one of those trophy shelves like Stella keeps all of her soccer trophies on. Or if it was a medal I could frame it in a cute shadow box with my Camp Itchy Bitey ribbon... *Focus, Malone. You're in it to win it today. Glide like the wind!*

I crane my neck up just a tiny bit, but I can't even see Elizabeth or Brianna in the lanes next to me. I must be killing it! I sort of want to turn my head back and see how far ahead I am, but that would slow me down and there's no way I'm going to blow this. Even from the bottom of the pool I can hear all sorts of yelling above the water, which must be the team rooting for me. It sounds like they're blowing horns! Usually I can't hear a thing when I'm this deep.

It's so encouraging that I sail all the way to the end of the pool without even coming up once for air. With my arms above my head, I race toward the surface of the water and pop out, ready to soak up all of that delicious, thunderous applause.

Chapter 5

When I Discover I'm Swimming with a Shark

There's no delicious, thunderous applause.

There's not even polite clapping.

In fact, nobody is moving or making a sound anymore.

The other three swimmers are still standing on their blocks, shivering and staring at me with their mouths open. *What the heck?* Hanging on to the side of the pool, I shake the water from my ears and lift my foggy goggles onto my head.

"What's up, guys?" I call out.

"That was a false start, Margaret," Coach bellows back. "If this were a meet, that would be an automatic DQ. Please get back to your block quickly. And this time, maybe wait until *after* I blow the horn."

"DQ?" I ask. *An automatic Dairy Queen?*

"*Disqualification!*" Coach roars. I nod and duck into the water, trying not to cry. This is so embarrassing. I'd like to just float here under the water, but I don't since that's not an option with everybody waiting for me. I'm totally out of breath when I climb back onto the starting block.

"On your marks, get set..."

I hit the water dead last after Coach blares that terrifying horn. I swim as hard as I can but this time it's different with other swimmers in the lanes next to me. At first I think I'm seeing things, but tiny Brianna seems to be way ahead of me. Then I notice that Elizabeth has left me in the dust too. Obviously it's because I started a little late. I'm sure I'll catch up. But those two are flying across the top of the water like they're sledding down an icy hill on a snow day. What in the world? I'm a good swimmer! And Elizabeth said she was terrible!

Everyone is out of the pool by the time I make it back to the starting blocks. Coach is bent way down and talking sternly to Brianna.

"O'Connor beat you by two seconds," he hisses

through clenched teeth. "Two seconds!" Brianna is biting her lip, looking like she's trying not to cry. "But you're both first heat, so you'll have plenty of opportunities to outswim her." Brianna nods and runs off to the locker room. Coach shakes his head angrily. I move over next to Elizabeth.

"Not that great of a swimmer, huh?" I say.

"Yeah, well, my dad is amazing. He actually won four gold medals at the Olympics…and my brother is really good too. Compared to them, I'm terrible," she whispers with a shrug.

"Wow! That's really cool! And I'd say you measure up just fine here," I tell Elizabeth, giving her a hip bump that almost knocks her over.

She steadies herself and says, "I really do love the water. Thanks for getting me to do this, Maggie."

"What are friends for?" I ask.

"Margaret Malone?" Coach calls me over, looking down at his clipboard.

"Yes, Coach?" I answer, wrapping my towel around my waist.

"Yeah, what was that?" Coach asks me.

"What was what?" I ask, confused.

"You swam *under the water*, Margaret," Coach reminds me, like I don't already know that.

"Yes sir, and you can call me Maggie, sir. And oh, that's how I get around in the water the fastest and since we were racing…"

"What's your best stroke?" Coach asks.

"Stroke? You know, I don't really like those," I explain and Coach just keeps looking at his clipboard. "They showed us 'the strokes' back at Camp Itchy Bitey, but honestly, they just slowed me down. So I usually just swim under the water since I'm also amazing at holding my breath. I won first place for that—beat out Willie Westheimer, who told everybody his lungs were twice the size of any adult human, which is a total lie, but—"

"Well, congratulations on your lung capacity, Margaret, er, Maggie, but that's not an option. You've got to pick a stroke and get good at it," Coach tells me.

"Wait, I made the *team*?" I ask, shocked.

"I need warm bodies out there and I'm short on those this year, so you'll be our second alternate," Coach tells me. "If two girls can't make it to a meet, you swim. But you come to all of the practices and meets either way. In the meantime, you've got a lot of work to do. First practice is tomorrow afternoon."

Right about that time, Brianna comes slinking out of the locker room.

"Brianna," Coach shouts. She looks up timidly. "I want you to work with Malone here. Fifteen minutes before and after every practice. It'll be good for you too."

"Yes, Dad," she replies, looking down.

Dad? Brianna is the coach's daughter?

"Um, thank you?" I say, since it's pretty clear neither of us has a choice.

"I'll take her to get a team suit," Brianna says. "Come on, Maggie."

We start heading toward her dad's office.

"Hey, Brianna, I really appreciate you helping me out," I say, struggling for words. "I mean, you're an amazing swimmer. Really great! Like, way better than me, although I do have that first-place award from Camp Itchy Bitey." Brianna says nothing, so of course I keep talking. "Hey, you're not upset that Elizabeth swam a little faster than you did, are you? It's just swimming. It's supposed to be fun, right?"

35

"Oh…yeah, Maggie," Brianna agrees, smiling and looking around the corner. "You're right."

And then just like that, sweetness and light turn to fire and brimstone.

"Here's the deal, Malone," Brianna says, yanking me by the arm and pulling me inside her dad's office. "I'm gonna teach you not to drown…maybe…and you're gonna convince your friend back there to quit the team and never come back. You'll be doing her a favor. You see, I don't want her here. And if I don't want her here, I'll make *both* of your lives miserable. I can promise you that. Tell her to pick another sport. Got that?"

"Wait, what?" I say, totally confused.

"Are you deaf? Speak any English?" Brianna says, her eyes all skinny. "Get. Your. Friend. To. Quit. The. Team. Or else." She adds sign language gestures to make her point. Wow.

I'm kind of in shock and don't know how to respond, but that's okay because Brianna has more to say.

"Listen, Malone, there is no end to the ways I can take her down," Brianna promises. "I've done it before and I'll do it again. It'll be an inside job, you see, my dad being the coach and all. The man believes every-thing I tell him, so you do the math."

I swear I didn't see her head spin around on her body, but it must have because I feel like I'm listening to the devil herself spin a tale of dastardly destruction. Even if I wasn't good at math, I think I'd get her gist.

"Well, um, Brianna?" I ask. "Why don't you just tell Elizabeth all this yourself?" It's kind of an obvious question, I think.

"Right!" Brianna huffs. "And have her go running to my dad and tell him how I threatened her? I don't think so. Either she picks another sport or I'll make sure she's DQ'd from playing any sport in this town again *ever*. Got it? Oh, and remember, I'll take you down with her." Brianna's bony little finger pokes me in the chest when she gets to this last part.

"Everything okay, girls?" Coach sticks his head into his office.

"Yeah, Dad," Brianna says brightly, turning and slinging swimsuits onto the floor. "Just finding the perfect fit for Maggie and explaining how things work around here."

I look out at the pool and see Elizabeth swimming

her heart out. It looks like she's totally found her thing. And she has no idea that this tiny minnow here is actually a shark. Out for blood. Maybe *literally*.

Chapter 6

When I Turn into a Big, Fat Liar

Elizabeth and I stuff our wet suits and towels into our backpacks and head down the hill on our bikes. As soon as we're safely out of earshot, she lets out a huge whoop.

"We did it!" she shouts—*shouts*! "We made the team! I mean, sorry about the alternate thing, but wasn't that nice of Coach to ask Brianna to help you? She's so cute, and she's actually a really strong swimmer! Oh, and I'll help you too, of course. We can swim on the weekends! It's going to be so great. Amazing, even!"

"Yeah, I don't know," I say hesitantly. "Do you think maybe yearbook would be even *more* fun? I heard the photographers get to use these really fancy cameras and get front-row seats at all the games and stuff. That would be pretty cool, don't you think? I mean, just because we made the team doesn't mean we *have* to do it or anything…" I trail off.

"Wait, what are you saying?" Elizabeth asks, confused.

"I mean, all those laps and not that it always has to be about the outfit, but have you seen the swim team suits?" I say, struggling to come up with reasons why we shouldn't do swim team, even though I'm the one who was all for it in the first place.

Elizabeth steers her bike to the side of the road and stops, so I do the same.

"I don't know," she says, thinking about it.

"And have you noticed the swimmers' hair? It's green, Elizabeth! *Green!* I don't know about you, but I wore a green wig the year I was a pumpkin for Halloween, and that was *not* a good look for me."

"I hadn't thought about that," she says, patting her shiny blond head absentmindedly.

"Besides, when we're on the yearbook staff, we can put all our friends on the Pinkerton Parade page," I add. "It's a definite perk of the job, you know. I just think swim team isn't the best fit for us." I nod my head for emphasis, relieved that the whole Brianna thing is going to blow over like a dark cloud that doesn't actually ruin your day at Wally World.

"Wait a minute, don't you mean for *you*?" Elizabeth asks, looking right at me like I just stole her last Oreo when she wasn't looking. "You mean swim team's not a good fit for *you* since you made second alternate."

"Oh, no, it's not *that*... I just..." I mumble, trying to come up with the right words, but I'm too late.

"You know what, Maggie? I think you're jealous that I made first string and so now you want to quit. Well, you can go right ahead, but I'm staying on the team."

"No, Elizabeth, you don't understand," I say, straddling my bike. "I'm not jealous, I promise. It's just that, well, Brianna is seriously going to make your life miserable if you stay on the team. She told me so herself."

Elizabeth laughs—not a happy laugh but a full-on angry laugh, if there is such a thing—and shakes her head.

"Yeah, right. That sweet little girl told you she's going to *make my life miserable*? Maggie, I don't

41

believe you. I thought you'd be happy for me, but I think you're just jealous. Have fun doing yearbook." She puts her helmet back on her head, like a neon sign telling me that she is DONE with this conversation.

"No, that's not it, Elizabeth," I plead. "I'm telling you the truth!"

I've got to somehow make her believe me! Her life might depend on it! Think, Malone, think!

"Hey! Do you remember hearing about that third grade girl who got her head shaved at a sleepover when she fell asleep first?" I ask, rolling my bike closer to hers.

"Yeah, so?" Elizabeth asks, looking at me sideways.

"That was Brianna!" I yell, arms wide for emphasis, hoping that will get her attention.

"It was not," Elizabeth scoffs. "That's some kind of urban legend. My second cousin in California told me *she* knew the girl who stole her dad's electric clippers and did that."

She's right. I made that up, but I've got to come up with something that will convince her to stay out of harm's way—Brianna's way. What's it going to take?

"She told me herself, Elizabeth!" I explain. "She

also told me that she put a bunch of Ex-Lax—you know, the stuff that's about a thousand times stronger than prune juice—in a Hershey bar wrapper last year and gave it to a girl on the swim team who was number one, when Brianna was number two, right before a meet. The girl pooped in the pool, Elizabeth! Talk about disgusting, and right in front of both teams and all the parents! It took weeks to drain and disinfect the Mountain View Pool!"

Whoa! Can I get some fries with that Whopper? I don't ever tell lies, but desperate times call for desperate measures. Besides, I'm doing it for her—not for me. That makes it sort of okay, doesn't it? I look at Elizabeth, hopeful that I've convinced her to abandon this swim-team madness.

"I never heard about that," Elizabeth says, looking skeptical.

"Oh yeah, it was a huge scandal," I say, hopping on my bike and giving her a smile. "So what do you say we just do yearbook?" I cross my fingers and say a silent prayer that my tall tales have done the trick.

"I say no thanks," she replies, staring me straight in the eyeballs. "I thought you were a real friend, but

43

I guess I was wrong. I think you're a liar." Before I can make sense of what just happened, she takes off toward her house.

"Wait!" I call after her—but she's gone.

I pedal home slowly and consider my options. As far as I can see, I have two: I could just quit the team and let Elizabeth fend for herself—but that leaves me back where I started, all alone in the nosebleed section at next week's pep rally. The other option is to get my friend to quit the team and think it was all her idea.

Misery loves company, right?

Chapter 7

When I Step into the Coolest Flippers Ever

When I get home, I stash my bike in the bushes, race to my room, and sit down at my computer. I start thirteen different emails to Coach King, but I delete them all. In one, I try telling him that Elizabeth's family is moving to China, but then I realize she'll just show up for practice on Friday so that won't work. In another, I let it slip that Elizabeth is failing Spanish, which would get her benched…only she's not failing. In fact, she's a straight-A student like me, so all she'd have to do is show him her report card.

Then I write that I think he should know that Elizabeth has the really bad kind of asthma where she could drop dead from any sort of exertion, so I thought he might want to take her off the team for her own good. That one's the worst—and I realize I just can't do it.

"It's so unfair," I say, slumping into my vanity chair and staring at my reflection in the mirror. "I *am* a real friend, and I'm *not* jealous! Well, maybe I am a tiny bit, but I'm not a liar. Okay, fine, I stretched the truth about Brianna with those crazy stories, but it was for Elizabeth's own good. Is it my fault she wouldn't believe me when I actually told her the truth? Oh, what am I going to do? How am I ever going to fix this?"

"Are you asking yourself or me?" Frank says.

"AAAAAAAAAAACCCCCCCCCCCCCCCC-CCCKKKKKKKKKKKKKKKKKKK!" I scream, tipping over backward in my chair. I land in a heap on my zebra rug, my heart pounding harder than it did the time my brother, Mickey, and his friend Oliver hid under my bed and waited until I was *this close* to falling asleep before they rolled out, jumped up, and shouted *Gotcha!* right into my face.

"Geez, Frank, could you give a girl some warning?" I ask, pulling myself back up into my chair.

"If I'm not mistaken, *you* called *me*." Frank-in-the-mirror laughs.

Frank came with the MMBs—Mostly Magical Boots—and the only way I can talk to him is in a mirror. That's why he's Frank-in-the-mirror. Anyway, since I haven't had the MMBs that long, I'm not always sure exactly how it all works. But this is definitely the first time Frank has just shown up like this, practically uninvited. Still, I'm pretty glad to see him. I need *somebody* to talk to.

"Well, since you're here and everything," I tell Frank, "you got any of that great genie advice you're so famous for? Just please don't tell me 'You've got this,' okay? Because I obviously don't. Like, at all." I let out a huge sigh. My heartbeat is slowing to a normal rhythm again, thankfully.

"Which part of this little mess do you want my help with?" Frank asks.

"Well, I… Wait, what's that clicking sound?" I ask, totally distracted by the noise.

Frank holds up a pair of knitting needles and a huge ball of bright blue yarn. "I'm making a beanie," he says. "What? Knitting relaxes me."

"You're weird," I tell Frank.

"Compared to all the other genies you know?" Frank asks with a laugh, click-clacking away.

"Whatever. I just don't know how to make Elizabeth believe me. Or what to say to Brianna," I explain, resting my chin in my hands.

"I hear you," Frank says, setting his knitting needles aside. "That little whippersnapper's a piece of work. Who peed in her Rice Krispies anyway?"

"Okay, that's just gross," I say, cringing.

"Here's the thing, Malone," he says, leaning in. "You can't control what other people do…or how they act, what they say, or what they believe. All you can do is be yourself. Stay one hundred percent Maggie Malone—you know the deal. Now that's some excellent genie advice, if I do say so myself." Franks nods, pleased with himself.

"But that bratty girl's going to—" I protest.

"Nope!" Frank holds up a hand to stop me.

"And Elizabeth thinks that I—" I plead.

"No, ma'am, Pam," Frank says.

"Wait, who's Pam?" I ask, confused.

"Oh, that's just something people say. You know, like 'Hop on the bus, Gus,' or 'Slip out the back, Jack,' or…" Frank continues.

"Not to be selfish, but I really don't feel like playing

48

a rhyming name game right now. As a matter of fact, all I really want to do is crawl under a rock and wait for all this to be over. Or sink deep down to the ocean floor, far away from this mess where the only things I can hear are dolphins and waves and… *Oh my gosh, that's it!*"

"What's it?" Frank looks up because apparently he'd gone back to his beanie.

"Marina Tide! I want to be her!" I explain, jumping up and throwing my hands over my head. "She lives in Florida… Well, technically she lives wherever her big boat takes her, but she's off the coast of sunny Florida right now, and it's freezing here so…I'll soak up the sun and swim with Skipper and probably save a coral reef! It's going to be amazing!"

"You know, her life might not be as easy or perfect as you think it is," Frank says.

"Yeah, right, Frank!" I laugh. "It'll be tough to decide which of Marina's seventy swimsuits to wear and to spend all day petting that adorable dolphin and getting a tan! And even if she has to clean the boat from top to bottom everyday, it has to be better than what I've got going on here. And since Marina's practically a fish herself, I can work on some of my strokes and maybe get bumped up to first alternate on the swim team. It's perfect timing, when you think about it."

"Well, the MMBs aren't for running away from your own life, you know," Frank tells me. "But I do agree that maybe you'll learn something as Marina that you can use to help you out with this little swim team…situation. Do you think you can keep your eyes open for that?"

"Oh, sure, definitely," I say, but I'm not really thinking about what he's saying. I'm too busy picturing myself exploring gorgeous coral reefs and body surfing alongside sweet little Skipper and, most important, *not* having to deal with Brianna the piranha for a day.

"Then I guess it's settled," Frank says. He looks at me a little sideways and then leans in toward me in the mirror. "Don't forget your trusty genie pocket mirror in the drawer there… I'm guessing there aren't a lot of mirrors on Flynn Tide's trawler."

"Right!" I say, relieved that he didn't try to talk me out of slipping into Marina's super-cool flippers for a day. "Good thinking, Frank! TTYL!" *There's no way he's going to get that*, I think to myself.

"*OK!*" Frank yells back, changing from a clear pic-ture in my mirror to a watery blob. "TTFN!"

I kind of love that genie.

Chapter 8

When I Wake Up in the Middle of the Ocean

Not to be full of myself or anything, but I'm kind of getting to be an MMB professional. Last night I laid out my clothes and set my alarm to go off extra early today. (I picked four forty-four because I love it when numbers repeat. On regular school days I always set it for five fifty-five, even though I don't technically have to be up until six fifteen. I'm sort of strange like that.) The alarm blares and I bolt straight up in bed. *It's showtime!*

I tiptoe into the bathroom to brush my teeth. Then I put on my favorite tracksuit, the hot-pink one with white stripes down the sides. Even though I won't be wearing it when I wake up as Marina, I feel sporty when I wear it so it seems fitting. Plus it has pockets so I have somewhere to stash my genie pocket mirror. I slip the mirror in the pants' side pocket and zip it up nice and tight. After giving my hair a quick scrunching—there's no sense trying to *comb* it or anything, since I'm sure it'll be wet in, like, five minutes—I walk over to my closet and pull down the MMBs from the tippy-top shelf. They smell like chicken curry mixed with burnt marshmallows. Don't ask me why, but they do.

I pull on the MMBs and stand up tall. Then I walk over to my mirror. I've got to tell you, beat-up old cowboy boots look pretty funny with my tracksuit, but I won't be wearing this crazy getup for long. "With these MMBs I choose," I say to my reflection, "a day in Marina Tide's shoes!"

* * *

Why is there water slapping up against my room? And why is it, like, seven hundred degrees in here, even though there's a fan blowing right on me and whipping my curls into a strawberry–blond tornado? That'll be fun to brush out… And the windows in my room have shrunk to tiny, round holes the sun is shining right through. Wait a minute! I'm her! Marina Tide!

54

I hear two hard knocks on the metal door to my room…er, Marina's room. "Swab the decks in five, sweetie!" I hear a man say, followed by footsteps down the hall. I'm guessing that was Marina's dad, Flynn. I'm not really sure how one swabs a deck, but I hope it doesn't involve Q-tips. I hop out of bed and walk all of two steps to Marina's tiny closet. Hey, everybody can't be a princess or a rock star, right? The room is rocking gently from side to side, and I have to grab hold of the closet doorknob to steady myself. I hope I grow a pair of sea legs today! Those would come in handy.

Marina's closet, if you can call it that, is just a few shelves with baskets strung together by bungee cords. I know it might sound silly, but I've been terrified of bungee cords ever since I heard about Stella's cousin Kenny, who used a bungee cord to pull his brother Benji on a skateboard behind his motorized scooter. Benji got a good ride at first, but then that bungee cord let loose and popped him right in the eyeball. *Ugh!* It makes me blink about a billion times just thinking about it. Luckily for Benji, his eyeball didn't roll out into the street and get squished by a truck. He did have to wear an eye patch for a while, but that was right when *Pirates of the Mediterranean* came out so he kind of liked it.

Squinting my eyes almost shut, I pull a bungee cord from its hook and plop a couple of baskets on the bed. As I suspected, she has all kinds of swimsuits, red ones with white polka dots, pink ones with turquoise trim, and one that's all rainbow-striped from top to bottom. That one is all me! I step out of my pajamas, and when I do, they make a big thud. I slip into the suit, then I pick the pajamas back up and feel around until I find my pocket mirror in the side pocket. Since there's nowhere to stash that thing when you're decked out in nothing but a rainbow swimsuit, I stuff it underneath the rest of the suits and return the basket to the closet. Shutting my eyes tight, I pull the bungee cord back and snap it into place.

I grab a big, fluffy white robe from a hook by the door and slip it on. It says *Sea Angel* in bright blue embroidery on the back and it's softer than a newborn bunny. I pull on the bedroom door handle—it's like a little ring, not a knob—but the thing is locked. I jiggle and jostle it, and I'm looking for an unlock button when I remember that on Uncle Winston's boat, you had to lift the door *up* to open it. It was a safety feature to keep those doors from flapping around in rough seas. I try it and it flies open, and when it does, I fall face-first into a giant step. *Mother of a slippery squirrel monkey, is this going to happen every single time?*

I brush myself off and look up a tall, ridiculously narrow staircase with railings on each side. It's actually more of a ladder than a staircase. I grab hold of those rails and pull myself up one step at a time. Each step is at least a foot high. I guess it's a good thing they make us do all of those lunges in PE, because even with all that training, I'm nearly out of breath when I hit the top of the stairs.

That's when I see it: miles and miles and miles of the bluest, most beautiful water I've ever set my eyeballs on. It's so clear and clean that it's almost *white* in places. I'm so overwhelmed by the sight that it takes me a minute to notice something else. There's not a sliver of land in sight! Just an endless world of water all around me. Which makes me panic. *We're lost at sea! WE'RE LOST AT SEA! Where are the life vests? The rescue boats? Why isn't anybody sending giant flares into the sky? We'll die out here in the middle of nowhere. DIE, I TELL YOU.* I'm gripping the sides of those rails for dear life when a voice startles me half to heaven.

"Morning, Marina!" a woman says, coming up behind me and ruffling my hair. It's a good thing I'm holding on or I'd have tumbled straight back down that ladder-staircase. "Just as soon as you get these decks swabbed you can do your morning mile. You might want to hurry too. Skipper's getting antsy." The woman is tiny for a grown-up—my mom would say, "petite"—and has long, straight hair that falls almost to her butt and looks to be naturally streaked blond by the sun. She's wearing khaki shorts and a *Sea Angel* T-shirt and has a ginormous camera on a strap around her neck.

She points to the boat's back deck and there, bobbing in the water not ten feet from me, is the world's most adorable dolphin. He's shiny and gray and has this sweet little white patch right under his chin. Do dolphins even have chins? I'm not really sure, but I'm almost positive he just smiled at me.

Chapter 9

When I Meet My New Best Surfer Friend

"Actually, Mare, you slept a little later than usual," the woman says, looking at her big, black, rubbery, must-be-waterproof-to-a-million-feet watch. "Captain Jack's been down in the galley for an hour so his famous 'flap-Jacks' are probably ready. Let's go grab a bite and then Zac can help you with those decks." *Can you say "score"?* I mean, flapjacks are probably one of my top ten favorite breakfast foods. (I think I have about thirty-seven.) And something about these MMBs makes me ravenous. I hope Skipper can hang in for a few more minutes. And I wonder who Zac is…

I follow the woman down a narrow alleyway that runs the outside length of the boat, holding tight to the side of the ship as I inch along. There's basically a clothes-line up here between me and all of that ocean below, and I'm not ready to make *that* kind of a splash.

"Morning!" bellows a man I'm guessing is Captain Jack as we enter the main cabin. He's wearing an apron over his own *Sea Angel* T-shirt and flipping pancakes on a griddle in the side of the room that looks like a kitchen—that must be the galley. He's got a big belly and a gray-speckled walrus mustache. You know, the kind where you can't tell if he's got any choppers in there? I decide to give him the benefit of the doubt.

"Don't be shy this morning," Captain Jack says, holding out a plate. "You've got a big day ahead."

"Thanks Captain Jack," I say, breathing in a face full of pancake deliciousness.

"Here you go, Lex," he says, offering a plate to Lexi.

"Give that one to Zac when he comes up," Lexi tells him.

"He's up," says a scruffy, mop-headed boy maybe a year or two older than me who shuffles into the room. He's wearing a *Sea Angel* T-shirt too—that must be the uniform around here—and he has that sandy-golden, sun-bleached hair the boys always have in surfer movies. Also? I wish Stella were here for an arm-by-arm comparison, because I think he might even be tanner than she is. The only kid we've ever met who is tanner than Stella was Mario Miceli, who was Italian *and* mowed lawns every day after school without a shirt in the spring and summer, so it didn't even count. If Stella did that, she'd turn the color of dark chocolate.

"Hey, Mare," incredibly tan Zac says to me as he slides into the chair next to me. "You look like cat puke today."

He says it with a big, friendly smile though, so I'm thinking we must be friends. Like the brother-and-sister kind of friends who give each other all sorts of grief but really like each other deep down. At least I'm hoping that's the case. It's about time I had an actual friend on one of these adventures.

"Thanks, Zac," I say with a smile, amazed at how calm I sound because Zac *is* pretty cute and I'm not always the coolest around boys. "You smell like a skunk that just ate anchovies and rolled in a pile of rotten eggs."

61

"Good one," Zac says with an appreciative nod. "When I'm a famous oceanographer someday, I might even keep you around." Jack and Lexi laugh. I shove a light and fluffy bite of flapjack into my mouth and smile with relief. We are friends! We're all friends! Today is going to be so great.

"Hey, your dad took the dinghy to scope out the reef for the photo shoot today, and he won't be back for at least an hour," Zac tells me through a mouth of flapjacks. "I'll do the decks so you can get to your warm-up."

An underwater photo shoot? Can you say totally awesome?

"Zac, first of all, *manners*," Lexi says with a big sigh. "And second of all, you know Flynn likes Marina to pull her weight around here."

"I know, Aunt Lexi," Zac says. "But I'm supposed to be the first mate, and that's the first mate's job! Besides, Mare here has a big day ahead of her. We don't want her getting all tired and cranky, do we?"

"Don't you have some logbooks to fill out?" Jack wants to know.

"Already done, Uncle Jack… I mean *Captain Jack*!"

Zac says, hand to forehead in an official military-like salute. Jack and Lexi smile at each other. "*And* I cleaned up the wheelhouse, checked the fuel levels and anchor lines, and charged all of the radios. I think we're good here."

Lexi laughs. "Fair enough, and that's sweet of you, Zac. But if Flynn flips out, it was all your idea."

"Deal," Zac says, giving me a big grin and a thumbs-up.

"Thanks, Zac, but maybe we could do it together," I offer, since it only seems polite. Plus I sort of need to get a grip on this "big day" ahead of me. "Maybe if we have time, we can go over the details of today's shoot. You know, give me the first mate's perspective on how it's all going to go down."

"Race you to the supply closet!" Zac shouts, pushing himself away from the table and bolting from the salon.

"No running!" Captain Jack shouts after him. But he's smiling when he says it, and you can tell that everyone around here is just about as awesome as they come.

Oh Maggie, I think, giving myself a mental pat on

the back as I scramble to catch up with my new buddy Zac, *Marina Tide might be your best choice yet.*

Chapter 10

When I Have My Own Swim-with-a-Dolphin Movie Moment

Zac pulls a couple of mops and buckets from a tiny metal closet. "Bow or stern?" he asks me and I figure we must have some really funny secret language because I have no idea what he's talking about.

"Zeep or chong?" I reply.

"What'd you just say?" Zac says with a sideways smile. He thinks I'm hilarious so I keep going, and this time I throw in some robotic arms.

"Dirp or tang?" I say, really getting into it this time with my robot moves.

"What the…" Zac looks really confused, and I can feel my face getting hot because I realize that there is no secret language and I'm a total ding-a-ling.

"Wait! I get it! You're doing the robot from that old *Lost in Space* episode we watched! Good one!" Zac continues. "But I think it was more like this: 'Greetings, earthling. Take me to your leader.'" Zac does the robot arms and cocks his head to the side.

Seriously, Malone? You just got super lucky. You don't want to blow this before you even get to dip your little toe in the water!

"Okay, so *bow*?" Zac asks, motioning to the front of the boat with a mop. "Or *stern*?" he asks, motioning to the back of the boat.

"Oh!" I say, finally remembering that those are the weird names for the front and back of a boat. "Bow, please!"

"Good choice," Zac says, handing me a mop. "You don't want to torture Skipper back there waiting on you. Are you sure he's not at least part golden retriever?"

"I know, right?" I say because that sweet little dolphin really does love me—er, Marina. Whatever.

We clean the deck of the boat, and Lexi comes up the stairs carrying a giant plastic bottle. "Have you kids put on your sunscreen yet?" she asks, setting it at the top of the steps.

Holy cannoli, I can only imagine all the shades of red I'd turn if I didn't lotion up. This Irish skin does not tan. It burns, peels, and freckles. Then does it all over again, in that order.

"No, ma'am. Thank you!" I say, pumping a huge handful from the bottle.

"Hey, Zac, when you're a world-famous oceanographer yourself, you're going to have to hire somebody to remind you to put this stuff on," Lexi says with a laugh.

"You planning to ditch me or something, Aunt Lexi?" Zac asks.

"Never," Lexi says, and I get little goose bumps all over my arms. I love that Zac's family is so awesome.

I take my time spackling myself with sunblock from head to toe. I'm still traumatized by the gnarly sunburn I got last summer when my family went to River World for the day. I was in such a rush to get into that wave pool that I missed about half of my body when I was putting on my SPF 70. I looked like a red-and-white zebra when we got home, and my mom made me soak in a bathtub filled with vinegar. *Pee-yoo!* It did take away some of the sting, but my skin stunk like salad dressing for a week.

"I'm ready for my swim!" I announce, but everybody has gone to work on their next chore. There sure seem to be a lot of chores on a boat.

I walk to the back of the boat—the stern!—lay my towel across the railing, and look at this dolphin that's going completely berserk. He's nodding his head, like, *Come on!* And I think he may even be foaming at the mouth, he's so jazzed for me to get in the water with him. It's hard to tell. Don't get me wrong—he's adorable, but can I tell you? Up close, he's *huge*. And kind of looks like a shark. This really is like a dream come true to get to swim with Skipper, but...but what if he takes one dolphin whiff of me, realizes I'm not really Marina, and rips me to shreds? What? It could happen!

Just then, Skipper dives into the water, comes back to the surface, and sprays me with that butthole thing on his head.

Ewww! There has to be some kind of poop or snot mixed in with whatever he just hosed me down with. As terrified as I am to jump in, the thought of being covered in slimy dolphin snot is even worse, so I gather up my courage.

"Okay, buddy," I tell Skipper. "Here I come!" I pinch my nose with one hand, cross the fingers on the other—you know, for good luck—and plunge into the water.

As fast as you can say *salty sardines*, Skipper tucks his nose under my right arm and we're off like a shot. Like, through the water really fast. This guy is massive and super muscular and his skin feels like rubbery silk, which I love. But I have to say I don't really see why this would be called "swimming with Skipper" since it's more like being dragged along like a forgotten bumper on a speed boat. It feels like somebody just opened up a fire hydrant. On my face. But I manage to crane my neck above the water for a gulp of air. Sweet, delicious air.

Luckily, before I swallow my weight in water, Skipper slows to a manageable speed, like only *half* the speed of light, and then stops. *Whew!* I catch my breath and see the buoy in the distance. Skipper nods at me.

"What is it, buddy?" I say, treading water and talking to this adorable dolphin that almost drowned me. If he did drown me, I'm pretty sure he'd save me too.

"*Eeee eee eee eee eee!*" Well, that's what he says. Again, he motions toward the buoy.

"What? You want to race?" I ask, and those must have been the magic words because Skipper totally flips his wig. Well, not literally, because he's a dolphin and dolphins obviously don't wear wigs. What I mean is he goes crazy again like a dog waiting for somebody to throw a tennis ball.

I guess I'm going to race a dolphin, I think to myself. And just to make it even more ridiculous, I'll try and do the butterfly—only the hardest stroke known to the swimming universe—because that's probably what Marina would do.

"All right, boy! Let's *go!*" I announce, throwing my arms over my head, and the most amazing thing happens: I glide through the water like an Olympian. For real. Up and over, down, then up again. It's like nothing I've ever felt before, and at the same time, it's like I've done this every day of my whole, entire life. I look to my right and there's Skipper beside me. I know, from experience, that he can go a lot faster, but he's choosing to stay by my side.

This is like a dream.

We reach the buoy in record time, and when we do, Skipper leans in and gives me a gentle nudge, like a dolphin hug. It makes me realize that I'm for sure not dreaming and that this just might be the single most fantastic moment of my life.

Chapter 11

When the Coast Guard Shows Up

I sense it before I feel it, and I feel it before I hear it: another boat. Skipper and I are splashing around, playing this game he must play with Marina where I hold my arms over my head in a giant V, and he dives really deep and then comes shooting to the surface before bursting through the half circle and flipping in the air. It's cooler than one of those shows at Ocean World, probably because I'm *actually in the show*. I clap and wave my arms, and he does it again and again and it's out-of-this-world awesome.

I squint and try to scope out the approaching boat. At first I figure it's Finn—my dad for the day—coming back from his reef exploration, but this isn't any dinghy.

This boat is *enormous*, bigger than the *Sea Angel* by two times at least.

Pirates! I think with alarm, looking around frantically and realizing there is nowhere to hide. Still, I duck my head behind the buoy and peer around the side. *Pirates aren't real, you dodo*, I tell myself, trying to forget Auntie Fi's story about the time she was kidnapped by pirates on the high seas. Fortunately she got away—apparently she was wearing a fabulous gold-and-ruby ring an Egyptian king had given her and she was able to buy her freedom with it—but still. I don't think my rainbow swimsuit is going to buy me much of anything if a boatload of pirates scoops me up.

The huge boat is about to reach the *Sea Angel*, and from my perch behind the buoy I can see it's some sort of official-looking boat with lights on the top, almost like a police boat. Just then I see Captain Jack and Lexi rushing to the back of the trawler. Captain Jack's got his hands full of some sort of equipment, and Lexi is waving her arms at him and whisper-yelling at him. Even from here I can see she's all red in the face. I see Captain Jack shove whatever was in his hands into one of the lockers that's hidden under the big cushions on the back deck, like he's hiding something. What would he be hiding, I wonder, and why?

I feel like I'm watching a movie, only without the delicious buttered popcorn and supersize Sprite. I watch as the big boat ties itself to the *Sea Angel* and slowly swings to the side. When it does, I can make out the words "Coast Guard" on the side. I want to cry with relief. They're the nice guys who come to help you when your boat is sinking or tell you when a big storm is coming. Grandpa Winston was in the Coast Guard—that's where he fell in love with the "Great Big Blue" as he liked to call the ocean.

I watch as three uniformed men step from the Coast Guard boat onto the *Sea Angel*. Lexi and Captain Jack rush to greet them, and now they're all smiles. Maybe I watch too many movies. I mean, why does my brain always race straight to the dark side? I should probably work on that. Captain Jack and Lexi were probably just cleaning up the place for unexpected guests.

I give Skipper the arm wave I've already learned means "Let's go!" and we race back to the *Sea Angel*. Again, I'm amazed by my grace and skills. (I can say that because they're technically not "mine.") I really am incredible! I sure wish Coach King—better yet, his bratty daughter Brianna—was here to see me!

"Do you folks have any idea how lucky you are?" one of the uniformed guys is saying as I reach the boat. "I mean, there are exactly two permits in the whole world to be anywhere *near* this reef, and you guys have one of them. Do you know who has the other one?"

Lexi and Captain Jack shake their heads.

"The Coast Guard!" The guy laughs. "Us! That's it. Just you and us, the only two boats who are allowed to be here for any reason, under any circumstances. We trust you won't abuse that privilege, right? Because it is a privilege. A pretty incredible one."

"Good morning, gentlemen," I say, pulling myself up the little ladder that hangs off the aft deck. (That's a dive platform attached to the back of the boat. I heard Zac call it that before. I'd have surely called it "that little wooden-deck-thingy-on-the-back" so I was happy to have this information.)

"Miss Tide," one of the men says, nodding in my direction, obviously aware of who I am. I nod back and give him my best Miss Universe smile.

"As I was saying," the other man says, clearing his throat. "Command is doing some maintenance on our radio communication this week, so we're switching call signs. You can get us on 1111 if you need anything."

Eleven-eleven—that's my favorite time of day. Stella and I make a wish every time we catch it on a clock. Speaking of Stella, I make a mental note to thank her for sending me the link to those Flynn Tide videos. I spent a whole weekend watching them, and I know the Tide family legacy inside and out, back to Great-Great-*Great* Grandpa Milton "the Marlin" Tide who was a First Sea Lord—that's like the tippy-top guy—of the British Royal Navy. It feels great to be prepared when you're put in a sticky situation.

The thing is, I have no idea how sticky this particular situation is about to get.

Chapter 12

When I Start to Get into the Swim of Things

I swing through the salon and down the stairs to Marina's stateroom like it's something I do every day. Sitting on the edge of the bed, I pull a cute pair of avocado-green terry-cloth shorts with an elastic waist over my rainbow-striped swimsuit. Then I find one of those button-down long-sleeved sun shirts that says *Sea Angel* on the pocket and put that on. I figure that's perfect.

I hear two short knocks on the door to my room.

"Hey, Mare, your dad's tying up and I think he could use a hand from his best girl," Lexi calls through the door.

"Be right there!" I yell back. She really seems great. I love that I picked a drama-free life this time.

I tie my wild mane into a loose braid and head up

the stairs. I recognize Flynn "The Fin" Tide as soon as I see him. I know he's at least as old as my dad, but I have to say this guy's got kind of a superhero or movie-star quality to him. Dark hair and skin, a big, white toothy smile, and he's got a big, square chin that would make Superman jealous.

"Marina!" he yells when he sees me and tosses me the line to his boat. "Today's the day! Your favorite— *Acropora cervicornis!*"

Say what? I don't remember anything about Flynn speaking a different language. I try to think fast.

"Oh! Um, yeah, Dad! You know nothing gets me fired up like a big, juicy bowl of…" I trail off because I've got nothing. *What in the world is he talking about?* Luckily, he's distracted by Lexi, who starts going over the shoot schedule with him as soon as he steps on the boat. He gives me a huge smile and a little tug on my braid, and goes back to listening to Lexi.

"Would you like some kelp milk on your big, juicy bowl of exotic coral?" Zac says with a laugh. He's inside the cabin lining up gear on a long table.

"Sprinkled with extra-sharp shark's teeth, please,"

I reply with a wink. *I just winked at a super-cute boy!* I bite the inside of my cheek—because that's what I do when I get nervous around a boy—and pretend to be extremely busy coiling and recoiling the dinghy rope into a perfect circle on the deck. At least I know what *Acropora cervicornis* is now!

"Hey, Marina?" Zac hesitates and then continues. "Would you mind taking a look at my creative writing essay with me? It'll only take a few minutes and I have to submit it online today. You're such a great writer, and I'm just not sure…"

"Of course," I say. Because for one thing, I happen to be pretty darn good with words, and also because Zac has the sweetest puppy-dog face.

He rushes to his stateroom and returns with a folder. We sit side by side on the banquette in the salon and I read his essay while he waits, obviously hoping I like it. I laugh out loud when I read the part about him riding on the back of his buddy's moped, holding a burrito in one hand and a slushie in the other.

"I think it's great!" I say, handing it back to him when I reach the end. "It's funny and really honest when you make fun of yourself—I love that part.

You might wind up being a famous writer. An oceanographer-writer, of course!"

Zac shoves the paper aside and grabs both my hands. "You really think so?" he asks, looking me straight in the eye, and then he gives me a huge hug.

Just to be clear, I've never had a boy grab my hand before—let alone *both* my hands—and then give me a big bear hug. I think I might melt like a snowman that showed up in the wrong season.

"What about you, Marina?" Zac asks, collecting his papers.

"What *about* me?" I say, willing my brain to stop feeling so fuzzy.

"Well, I mean, I guess it's pretty clear that you're going to take over for your dad someday," Zac says. "I just wondered if there was anything else you wanted to do…or something you would do if your future wasn't already set in stone."

It's so sweet that he wants to know this about me—well, about Marina—but I'm afraid to answer for her! Like, what if I said, "Oh, I'd love to be an astronaut or an Olympic sprinter or a goodwill ambassador to Africa," and Marina's secret fantasy is to be a kindergarten teacher or a drummer in a rock band? That could make for some seriously awkward conversations between these two, and I'd hate to be the cause of *that*. Zac would be all, "But you *said* you wanted to be a fill-in-the-blank!" and she'd be all, "Uh, I never said that!"

"I guess I've never really thought about it," I tell Zac. "But I love that you asked me that! I'm going to start to think about it for sure."

"You should," he tells me, nodding his head enthusiastically. "Because you're amazing, Marina. For real. You could do anything you wanted. You know that, right?"

I'm flustered by his sweet words for a second, but then I remember something my mom always says: It's just as important to be able to accept a compliment as it is to give one.

"Well," I tell Zac, whipping out the best compliment response I've got, "coming from you, that means a lot." We sit there grinning like fools together, and it's all I can do *not* to tell him how glad I am that I picked a day in Marina Tide's shoes.

Chapter 13

When Things Get Fishy on the Sea Angel

"Sandwiches will be ready in five," Captain Jack announces. No fish tacos? Rats! I'd sort of gotten my heart—and my taste buds—set on having a couple of those, what with all the fish swimming around here, but maybe oceanographers don't eat fish. I guess that would make sense.

We all sit around the big wooden table on the aft deck, and Captain Jack serves everyone a turkey sandwich the size of an entire loaf of bread. I eat every last bit of mine—even though he put those spicy pepper flakes that make me sneeze on it—because that swim made me crazy-hungry.

"Look at Mare go!" Zac laughs as I inhale my sandwich.

"You might sink straight to the bottom of the ocean this afternoon with that much food in your belly!"

"Oh, don't worry. She's going to work it off," Lexi says. "There's still plenty of scrubbing to do around here. All of the vent screens need to be washed. The fluids need to be checked and topped, and every valve cover bolt needs to be inspected and tightened." Zac groans but he's smiling when he does it. You can tell he loves everything about being on this boat.

Maybe it's because they're different chores than I do at home, or maybe it's because I have Zac alongside me, whistling all sorts of silly, made-up tunes, but the time seems to fly. Zac makes a great chore partner and I find myself wishing—especially after that little chat we had before lunch—that I had some guy friends like Zac back at home. Not that I'm looking to replace Stella or Elizabeth or Alicia or anything, but there's something just plain cool about hanging out with a guy. I decide I'm going to work on that.

"Not half bad," Zac says, inspecting my work.

"Thanks," I say shyly, turning away. When I do, I see Captain Jack climbing the ladder onto the stern. He's wearing full scuba gear and being super quiet for the big guy he is, until he accidentally trips over a rope I just coiled. He stumbles and flails, and instead of freeing himself, he gets all caught up in the rope. Captain Jack tries to steady himself by grabbing on to a bunch of life vests hanging on hooks. I cover my mouth when he pulls the whole mess of them down with him when he falls. The commotion brings Flynn and Lexi running.

"Jack, are you okay?" Lexi asks, all out of breath. Jack nods and shakes his head, which sends water flying everywhere.

"You've been diving this afternoon?" Flynn asks, helping him up. "You know we have a limited number of dives in the area so that we keep our disruption of the ecosystem minimal."

"Surface dive only, Flynn," Jack explains, hanging the life vests back on the hooks. "This mask was leaking and I had to test the regulator—valve's been acting up. We're all set now."

"Relax, Flynn," Lexi says to Flynn in kind of a baby-talk voice. You know, that voice where it sounds like somebody's being really sweet to you, but really they think you're kind of dumb. Why would she speak like that to him? He's only one of the most famous oceanographers in the world. He doesn't seem to notice. "Captain Jack knows what he's doing."

"Oh, of course. Right," Flynn says, shaking his head and focusing on Lexi's clipboard. "Sorry, I'm just a little nervous or excited, I don't know. It's my little girl's first solo shoot and…"

"I know," Lexi says, comforting him. "I've watched her for a year and a half, and I can tell you that she's absolutely ready. I don't think anybody in the world knows more about staghorn coral than Marina Tide. And in the post-dive interview, she'll be able to explain, in words that kids across the country can understand, how important it is to protect this endangered species."

"You're right," Flynn agrees. "It'll be great. Zac, why don't we go down to your stateroom and go over your notes for the shoot one more time?" Zac nods and follows Flynn.

As soon as they're gone, Lexi turns to me.

"Marina, this is a deep dive today, so get your full suit and booties on, okay?" she says.

"You got it!" I tell her, hoping I can find the

right suit down there. Then I remember Marina's microscopic closet and figure it won't be too tough of a task.

"Jack, I need to talk to you for a second," I hear Lexi say as I tuck into the main cabin. I know it's not polite to eavesdrop, but I'm still a newbie in Marina Tide's life and I need some inside scoop on my dive and shoot plan here. I crouch below one of those little round windows and listen.

"What was that?" Lexi whispers to Jack. "You were supposed to be back on the boat making lunch before Flynn got back!"

"We agreed the kid shouldn't handle the dynamite, right?" Jack says. "It had to get down there somehow."

Did I just hear *dynamite*?

"I'm scared, Jack," Lexi says. "I just don't know if I can go through with it."

Go through with WHAT?

"It's a little late for that, Lexi." Captain Jack's voice turns angry. "Listen to me. We joined this team and came here for one reason: to find that buried treasure. The treasure that my father spent his whole life searching for and died trying to get his hands on."

89

"But do we really have to blow up the reef?" Lexi pleads.

"We've tried everything else, Lexi. You know that," Captain Jack says. "We're talking about my father's legacy, and I'm not leaving here without it. We stick to the plan. Got it?"

GULP! What. Is. Going. ON?

Chapter 14

When I Realize the Timer Might Be Ticking

My head is swimming—pun intended—when I get down to Marina's stateroom. *Buried treasure? That somebody DIED trying to find? And stick with the plan? WHAT plan?* If ever there was a genuine, full-blown, I-need-a-genie crisis, this would be it.

"Frank!" I whisper into the tiny mirror on the back of Marina's stateroom door. "Earth to Frank! More specifically, *big, huge ocean* to Frank! Frank the Genie, please come in! This is a maritime EMERGENCY! S.O.S!"

"Well, if it isn't Maggie-Marina-Tide-Malone," Frank says, his face coming into focus in the mirror. "You sound like a girl who just found a family of ants camping out in her pajamas! Or should I say a cluster of sea slugs in her wet suit?" Frank says this with a belly laugh, but I am *not* in the mood.

"Frank, something crazy is happening," I tell him, ignoring his joke—and the fact that he's wearing what looks like a bullfighting costume.

"Crazier than diving into somebody else's life midstream, you mean?" Frank laughs again, neatly adjusting a fringy gold tassel on his shoulder. Of all of the genies in the world, I had to get one who thinks he's the star of his own one-man comedy show.

"Like, major big-time crazy," I tell him. "I think Lexi and Captain Jack are planning something… something *bad.*"

"Maggie, remember what I told you about Brianna, because it applies in this life too," Frank says with a sigh. "You can't control what other people are going to do. Worry about your own self."

"I *am* worrying about my own self, Frank," I say nervously. "I'm worried that these *other people* are planning to do something really scary and dangerous that's going to kaboom my own self!" My heart is pounding inside my chest.

"Well, if that's true, then I guess you have to ask

yourself what Maggie Malone would do. I think Maggie Malone would find someone she could trust and tell them about this majorly scary business you speak of," Franks says, distracted, leaning back and forth in a cloud of smoke.

"I mean, I *think* I heard them say… But what if I'm wrong? They seem so nice… I don't know," I explain, confused and hoping for a good genie answer.

"Look, Mags, I'd love to chat more but they're about to release the bulls," Frank shouts. "Go with your gut! Do some digging. Ask some questions. Remember, *you've got this*! And let's hope I've got this too, or you may be in the market for a new genie!" I watch in frustration as Frank's face bounces up and down and fades away.

I can't control what other people are going to do? No kidding! Worry about my own self? Yeah, that's not hard to do right now. This is not exactly a first-rate genie revelation. He wasn't even listening to me! *Why, oh why, oh why* did I pick this life? And why don't MMBs come with some sort of warning? You know, like *Be careful what you wish for*, or something— anything—that might make you think twice before jumping into something that might not be at all what you expected.

I really have no choice, so after pacing around the tiny stateroom a few times, I finally pull the thickest, longest wet suit out of the closet and try to step into it. Now I know what a sausage feels like when it's getting stuffed! You know how when you're still wet from the shower and you try to pull your jeans on and those things are all "Yeah, that's not happening, sister"? Well, if this wet suit could talk, that's what it would be saying to me right now. Was I supposed to spray myself with cooking spray before attempting this?

I manage to get both feet into the ankle holes, and then I pull and I tug and I do about thirty-seven frog squats until finally I have the wet suit up to my waist. When I try to get my arms into it, I realize I've got the thing on backward! Who puts a zipper in the *back* of something, anyway? I peel it off and start the whole process all over.

I'm dripping sweat by the time I get the thing zipped up—which is no easy task itself, because I have to dance and shake all over the place to reach the long zipper strap in the back. That was not fun—but at least it distracted me for a few minutes from the mess I'm in. *Uncle of a salty sea urchin, the mess I'm in!* I take a gigantic breath to steady my nerves before heading up the stairs, because what else am I going to do?

When I get to the top, I can see everyone else— Flynn and Zac and Lexi and Captain Jack—in a huddle on the back deck. It looks like they're going over one of Zac's logbooks. I keep my eyes on the group as I tiptoe over to Lexi's dive equipment lined up on the big table. There are three different cameras, some funny-looking computers on wrist straps, and a stretchy belt that must weigh at least ten pounds. I pick up one of the computers. It's got a round dial with a bunch of numbers on it that mean absolutely nothing to me, and I can feel my knees start to shake. *I'm about to go scuba diving, in the ocean, and I have no idea what I'm doing. Scuba diving is dangerous, deadly even, if you don't know what you're doing! I sure hope Skipper has my back, because I'm not so sure anybody else on this boat does.*

I pick up a plain, black, waterproof box from the table. It's about the size of a fat book, and it says OTTER on the top in all capital letters. Oh, I love otters! They might be my second-favorite sea animal, after dolphins of course. We went to the River Bend Aquarium on a school field trip last year, and I got picked out of the whole audience to dole out the dead-fish treats during the otter show. Those dead fish smelled as nasty as you'd think, but it was totally worth it because I got to go backstage and pet those sweet little critters. I thought they'd feel all rubbery like Skipper, but they were covered with thick, soft fur.

On the way out, they gave me a giant stuffed version of Otto, the River Bend mascot. But wouldn't you know, Izzy Zimmerman turned green with envy and stole that thing right out of my backpack on the bus ride home. When we were walking off the bus, I was all, "Um, Izzy, that's my Otto." Hello, his head was sticking out of *her* backpack. And she was all, "Uh, no it's not!" Can you believe that? In the end, I just let her have it. Anybody who knew Izzy knew it wasn't worth it. She once gave Willis Freedman a black eye just because he wouldn't give up his banana-cream pudding cup at lunch.

I turn the box over in my hands, wondering what's

inside it. Maybe it's fish food…or more film…or a first-aid kit? I check outside and see the crew is still in a tight little huddle, so I pop open the lid.

It's definitely not fish food…or more film…or a first-aid kit. It looks some sort of timer. One that's speeding backward, ticking off the seconds, even as I hold it in my sweaty hands. I'm no expert, but it might be the sort of timer you'd use to activate a bunch of dynamite you put underneath a precious coral reef that you were planning to blow up.

Chapter 15

When Things Go from Bad to Worse

I hold the otter box in my hands, wondering if there can be any other explanation. Maybe I really did hear them wrong. Maybe they were talking about some *Scooby-Doo* episode they saw once, and not about actually blowing up this spectacular reef we're supposedly here to protect. Maybe I was dreaming, or maybe the salt air has gotten inside my skull and my brain's all crusty so I think I'm hearing things I'm not. Flynn and Zac have gone back down to the salon. I can see Lexi and Captain Jack on the aft deck with their heads really close together, so I drop to my hands and knees and crawl over to where I can hear.

"She'll be safely back on the boat before it blows, Lexi," Captain Jack is whispering.

"And *then* what?" Lexi asks.

"And then we'll have my grandfather's treasure and be rich beyond our wildest dreams," Jack says.

"Marina?" It's Zac. He must have just come up the stairs into the salon. The kid sure knows how to sneak up on a person.

"Hey!" I shout way too loudly. "You scared me!"

"What are you doing on the ground like that?" Zac wants to know. Well, it's a legitimate question since I'm on all fours looking like a Labrador retriever. I stretch up to peer out at Jack and Lexi, who are looking back at me like they want to know the same thing.

"Oh, I was just doing my stretching," I say, pushing myself up into a downward dog. "It's good to limber up before a dive, you know. You guys should try it!" I'm panting pretty hard, from nerves and also from trying to talk upside down.

"What did you just hear?" Captain Jack barks. Lexi puts her arm on his.

"He means," Lexi says, "did you hear us going over all of the details, or do you need us to go over them again?" Captain Jack's face is redder than an over-ripe tomato.

"Um, could we go over them again?" I ask. My heart is slamming against my rib cage and I hope they can't hear it, although I doubt that. In my head it sounds louder than when I put my sneakers in the dryer.

Captain Jack nods, but he does *not* look happy. "We'll be there in five minutes," he says. "Be ready to go."

"Wonder why he's so moody today," Zac whispers. "Maybe he's nervous about this dive."

"He wouldn't be the only one," I whisper back, taking a deep breath. Auntie Fi says that's the fastest way to calm your nerves, and my nerves could use some serious calming.

"You? Marina Tide, nervous? I'm not buying it." Zac gives me *that smile* and I melt just a little.

"Zac, are your aunt and uncle...you know... Do you think they would ever hurt the reef?" I ask.

"Hurt the reef? Are you *crazy*?" Zac says with a laugh. "They wouldn't hurt a single hair on a mermaid's head if you paid them."

"Right," I say. I want him to be right so badly it hurts.

"Why would you even ask that?" Zac wants to know.

"It's just...I heard them say something about the reef..."

"What about it?" Zac wants to know.

"I'm pretty sure it was something about...well, about blowing it up."

"Blowing it up?" Zac says, narrowing his eyes at me. "What do you mean?"

"Like...with dynamite," I tell him. "To get to some buried treasure."

"That's the most ridiculous thing I have ever heard," Zac says.

"Then what's this?" I ask, handing him the box with the timer in it.

Zac picks up the box and inspects it.

"Open it," I tell him. He does.

"It's obviously some sort of timer," he says, snapping the box shut. "Probably for one of the cameras. My aunt is a professional photographer, you know." His face looks like it's on fire, and I wish I could take it all back.

"I probably heard them wrong," I say, scrambling to change the subject. "I do that all the time! You know that song that says 'put your past away'? I always thought it was 'the butcher passed away.' I mean, that would be an awful line for a song, right?"

"I can't believe you'd think something bad about them for even a second," Zac says. "I thought we were friends." He storms off down the stairs and I'm left shivering at his words. But I can't worry about my friendship with Zac right now. I have to tell Flynn. There's no other choice. If I don't, I'm pretty sure the endangered coral reef he's so keen on protecting is in serious danger of being blown to Bangkok and back any minute. I rush out to the deck.

"Flynn? I mean, Dad?" *Don't blow your cover now, Malone!* I slow down and take a breath. He's sitting with Lexi.

Rats.

"Marina!" Flynn says, wrapping me in a big bear hug. "Just the girl I wanted to see. It's almost time for your dive. You ready?"

I sort of nod, because what else can I do?

"It's time for you to step out on your own now, without me. But I'll be right here waiting to hear all about it. Of course, your buddy Lexi here is going to be your dive partner for the shoot," Flynn tells me. "You know what that means… You two stick together no matter what." Lexi just stands there and smiles like she's not wicked Queen Matilda from the Mini Mermaid movie, which she totally is.

"That's right, Mare. It'll just be you and me down there," Lexi says, pulling me from Flynn's arms. "We're going be a great team." *What are we calling our team, Lexi? The Coral Dynamos?* I try to fake a smile, but I'm not good at that. The corners of my mouth don't want to turn up.

"I think I need to hit the restroom one last time," I say, stalling. Well it's not like I can say I need an emergency genie conference, is it?

"Make it quick," Flynn says. I give him a thumbs-up and practically slide down the steep staircase. I lock myself in the bathroom.

"Fffffffrank!" I whisper-yell into the metal plate that looks almost like a mirror since I am in full-on panic mode now. "Kinda need you right now! I'm about to be blown to bits! You can ignore me the next three times I call you, just not this time! Come in, Frank!" His face starts to come into focus but I can't really see or hear him all that well since this piece of metal isn't exactly a mirror.

"Maggie! How…doing?" he asks, squinting his eyes to see me. "Is this the best mirror you could find?"

"Sorry! Just listen!" I say, because I really don't have much time. "It's true! I definitely heard Captain Jack and Lexi talking about blowing up the reef! With dynamite. You know, *boom, boom*? And I'm pretty sure that little box I'm supposed to carry down there today has the timer inside it!"

"Okay, Mags. I'm only catching about every third word you're saying. I definitely heard dynamite and *boom, boom*," Frank says, getting serious like I've never seen him. "Sounds like you're in over your head. What's your plan?"

"Plan?" I ask, practically in tears. "I don't *have* a plan! Well, actually I do. It's to *not* get blown up today! Got any ideas?"

"Maggie Malone," Frank says. "If there's one thing I know about you, it's that you're a smart cookie. You'll figure it out. Did you talk to Zac?"

"I tried," I moan. "But he got really mad. I'm not sure he's even *speaking* to me anymore."

Frank looks like he's thinking about this. "What about Flynn?" he asks hopefully.

"I can't get him alone!" I shout, jumping up and hitting my head on the ceiling of the tiny bathroom. "And I can't tell him in front of Lexi or Captain Jack—"

I can see Frank's lips moving but I can't hear a word of it. It's like I'm watching a MeTube video with the volume turned down—but there's no volume on this stupid metal plate!

"Frank?" I plead. "Frank, speak up! I can't *hear you*!"

Nothing.

Okay, Malone. Think. There's no getting to Flynn. Who else can I talk to? It's not like I know a lot of people out here in this huge ocean. It's just the *Sea Angel* and… *the Coast Guard*! I'll call the Coast Guard! They gave us their call number when they were here. One-one-one-one. Eleven-eleven. I just have to get to the radio without anyone seeing or hearing me and give them a jingle. Easy peasy!

I slide out of the bathroom, closing the door softly behind me, and run on cat feet past Zac's bedroom. He's blaring some kind of music with crazy drums.

That helps! I pass the tiny kitchen and haul myself up the ladder to the fly bridge where the radio is.

"What are you doing up here?" Captain Jack asks as I reach the top. He's hunched over a map, which he quickly folds and shoves under a logbook when he sees me. "Lexi's all tanked up and ready to go—she's waiting for you on the dive platform. We're on a tight schedule here, Marina, and we don't have all day. Now quit dillydallying and *get your butt in that water*."

Yikes. My butt's about to be in water, all right. *Hot* water.

Chapter 16

When I Take a Dive with Ursula the Sea Witch

"Grab your fins and I'll help you with your tank," Lexi says, all kittens and sunshine. I'm shaking like a skinny, wet dog. I pick up a pair of pink fins and step into one and then the other. I have to take giant, marching-band kick steps so I don't trip over the tips as I cross the deck.

"Uh, you know you can wait until you get in the water to put those on." Lexi laughs. *Laughs! Who can laugh at a time like this?* "There's nothing to be nervous about, honey. Today is going to be a breeze. You're ready."

Nothing to be nervous about, huh? *I don't know about you, Lexi, but I don't go around blowing up endangered coral reefs every day!*

Skipper is in his usual spot by the stern and he's as amped

up as ever. He sees me and does one of those standup tail scoots, nodding his big head the whole time. At least I have *him* on my side. I can see Captain Jack watching us from the fly bridge, and Zac is nowhere in sight. Except for Skipper, it really is just me and Lexi. I sit down on the dive platform, my legs and fins dangling in the water, and Lexi hauls a tank up and onto my back. This thing must weigh a hundred pounds! She straps me in and seems to be checking out all of my equipment.

"Okay, you're all set," Lexi says. I just nod. "Oh! I almost forgot! You'll need to take the sonar unit this time," she says, handing me *the box*. The box with the ticking timer in it. *Oh no she didn't!*

"The sonar unit?" I say with a gulp, clutching the otter box with shaking hands.

"Yeah, when we get down below the reef, you're going to find a nice safe spot to tuck it, but very carefully, you know, so you don't hurt the reef," she tells me, slipping into her own tank and fastening a thousand buckles and hooks. "We're going to use it to take some measurements—Captain Jack has a receiver up there on the fly bridge—and then we'll come back and get it in a few days."

"Does…my dad know about this?" I ask, stalling for time.

"Well, of course he does, silly," Lexi says dismissively. "He's the boss. But to be honest, he doesn't *love* the idea of us getting as close to that reef as we need to get to place it, so you probably shouldn't mention it. You know, just so you don't upset him. But he's totally on board. He knows that we're all here to do what's best for that reef." She nods her head a lot when she says this last rotten, stinking lie.

"What exactly are we…measuring?" I ask her.

Lexi pretends she doesn't hear me as she slips a strap around her neck that's attached to a huge camera. "I'm going to get some great pictures of you placing it too, and then in the video you can explain how this is an important part of an oceanographer's work!" *Pictures of* me *placing it?*

"But wait, Lexi, what are we—" I try to ask again, but she plunges right into the water. I wait for her to pop back up, but she's sinking—ever so slowly— deeper. Skipper is shaking his head frantically—*Let's go already*!

I consider my options: refuse to get in the water…

111

and have to deal with Captain Jack. And if he's about to blow up an entire coral reef, I'm pretty sure he's not someone I want being furious at me. I could "accidentally" leave the box with the timer in it behind… but Lexi would just make me come back for it. Finally I decide I only have one choice: go along with this horrible plan and then find a way to reach the Coast Guard ASAP. It's all I've got. Talk about the least of all evils!

I adjust my mask and put the mouthpiece end of the tube that's connected to my air tank into my mouth. I breathe in and out and realize I sound exactly like Darth Vader. I try to whisper "Luke, I am your father" but it's really hard to talk into this thing. The air feels freezing cold in my mouth and has a weird metallic taste. *This is what pure terror tastes like*, I think to myself, positive I will never forget it. Pinching my nose and hoping for the best, I slip the strap of the awful otter box onto my wrist and plunge into the crystal-clear water.

Whoooooooooa, this is crazy! I feel like I'm floating in space! I spin around like a ballerina and Skipper is right there beside me, his entire body undulating.

One tiny kick of my powerful fins and I fly through the water, just like Skipper. I can see forever down here, and the only sound I hear is my crazy breathing. There are schools of fish all around me—bright blue and yellow ones and little shiny, silver ones and big, brown spotted ones—darting this way and that. A turtle the size of my bed pillow glides right past me, and it's like I'm in this crazy underwater movie. It's magical and amazing and I could do this forever—except for the part where you can't talk, because that would make me bonkers. Oh yeah, or the part where I'm about to blow up a reef. Party over.

Skipper takes off and I follow him. He leads me over to Lexi. She gives me a thumbs-up and a nod when she sees me, like "Everything okay?" *Oh yeah, Lexi, everything's just peachy!* I give her the thumbs-up back—because what else can I do?—and she snaps a bunch of photos. Then she points down with three sharp jabs of her fingers and takes off toward the deep, dark water without even turning around to see if I'm following. Some dive buddy!

I catch up to her with no problem. We dive deeper and deeper, and it's like I've been a deep-sea diver my entire life. The water gets colder and darker every few feet and the fish get bigger. I do love the feeling of flying through this water! If only I could forget about the box that's strapped to my wrist. As I swim deeper, I feel my head getting tight, just like it does on an airplane. I plug my nose and blow really hard, and my ears pop right away. That's a major relief. Not that I can hear anything down here anyway, but it's no fun feeling like your head is wrapped in a thick cotton sock.

Lexi suddenly stops. She's hovering a few feet above the most beautiful bed of coral you could ever imagine. It's got bright blue fingers reaching up toward the surface and red fan-like arms waving gently back and forth. There are clusters that look like human brains and knotty bits that could be dried lava, and the whole thing is dotted with black blobs that have a million long spines jutting out in every direction. It's like a whole hidden world down here—and it's here all the time, all around the earth, at the bottom of every ocean! I'm so mesmerized by it that it takes me a minute or two to figure out that Lexi is trying to tell me something.

She points to me, then holds up her wrist, then points to the reef.

Super big gulp. Apparently it's time to unload this ticking timer.

Chapter 17

When I Realize Zac Has My Back

Lexi is holding her camera with one hand and motioning like *Hurry up, already!* with the other. Can I tell you how awful it feels to be a pawn in somebody's worse-than-awful scheme? It reminds me of bratty Brianna getting me to do her dirty work, trying to get Elizabeth to quit the team, only on a much, *much* bigger scale. If I drop this timer and the dynamite Captain Jack put down here explodes, this gorgeous reef that took about five thousand years to form (that's not an exaggeration—we learned that in school) and all the millions of sea creatures that live in and around it will be blown to smithereens. And all for money—some stupid treasure they *think* is somewhere around that reef. *Okay, you witchy woman. I'll drop this box, but I'll find a way to fix this before the damage can be done.* I've got time, right? And I'm sure Flynn has the exact coordinates of where we're diving. I've just got to get to that radio and call the Coast Guard. And fast.

I carefully tuck the box next to the reef like Lexi instructed. She gives me a thumbs-up and takes a zillion more pictures, then she points to the surface. I nod and follow her slowly back up toward the sunshine and hang on to the side of the sea buoy marking our dive spot. Skipper stays right by my side.

"Great job, Mare!" Lexi says after she pops out her mouthpiece. "Really great." She pushes her mask up onto the top of her head. I give her a weak smile, and she takes off swimming back to the big boat. She gets there before me and helps me off with my tank so I can climb up onto the dive platform.

"My girl nailed it, did she?" Flynn asks proudly as we haul our gear onto the boat. He's up on the fly bridge with a pair of binoculars around his neck.

"I knew it!" he shouts, raising his arms above his head. "I knew you would, Mare. Of course, you were down there with the best...so thanks to you too, Lexi." *Yeah, Lexi. Thanks a whole heaping lot!*

Captain Jack is on the aft deck waiting to help us into the boat. He holds out his hand to haul me up and I really, *really* don't want to take it, but there's no way I'm getting out of this water and into the big boat by myself on my Jell-O legs, so I do. But I'm not happy about it.

Zac comes up behind him with a towel.

"You okay, Marina?" he asks, throwing the towel around my shoulders. "You look a little pale."

Um, I thought we weren't friends anymore since I accused his precious aunt and uncle of being ruthless treasure hunters who blow up coral reefs to get what they want!

"I'm fine, you know, just…beat," I say, unzipping my wet suit like a pro. *How am I going to get up to that radio without anybody seeing me? Think, Malone. You've got a big brain. USE IT.*

"Maybe you should go lie down for a bit," Zac says, handing me a bottled water.

"Thanks," I say, taking the water and slurping half of it down in one huge gulp. I can taste the salt on my lips but still, water has never tasted so delicious. "Maybe I will." *Maybe there's a radio down there somewhere! There has to be. There just has to be.*

119

Zac walks over to the side of the deck, like he's looking for something, and then he comes back. He's acting all fidgety and weird. Maybe he *is* still mad at me.

"That's a great idea," Lexi pipes in. "I'm going to go download these photos and see what we've got. I think you're going to be really happy, Flynn."

"I'm not sure I could get any happier," Flynn says, jumping down from the fly bridge and giving me a big high five.

"Um, Jack?" Lexi says suddenly in a little-girl voice. "Did you radio for the Coast Guard?" Lexi points out toward the ocean, and sure enough, the enormous Coast Guard boat is barreling toward us.

Captain Jack looks like he's just seen a ghost. "Of *course* I didn't—I mean, why would I call the Coast Guard?"

"Well, then why are they coming this way in what looks like a big rush?" Lexi asks, sounding equally panicked.

"I called them," Zac says, looking straight at me.

Maybe we're friends after all.

Chapter 18

When the Truth Bubbles to the Surface

"Why'd you call the Coast Guard, Zac?" Flynn wants to know, looking very confused. Zac looks like he's trying not to cry. It might be the saddest thing I have ever seen.

The Coast Guard boat whooshes to a halt beside the *Sea Angel*, which starts bobbing and tilting in the enormous swells. "Maritime law grants us permission to board this vessel," one of the guards calls out through a loudspeaker. "Nobody move."

"Lexi? Jack? What is *going on*?" Flynn wants to know.

"That's exactly what we'd like to know," says the first guard to hit the deck.

"My aunt and uncle," Zac starts, pointing at Lexi and Captain Jack who both have their heads bowed in shame. "They're not who you think they are, Flynn. Not even close."

"What does that mean?" Flynn bellows, looking from one of them to the other. "Who are they then?"

Zac grabs my hand and gives it a squeeze. "Marina, do you want to tell him or do you want me to do it?" His sad face is ripping a big, huge hole in my heart.

"They're treasure hunters, Dad, not conservationists," I say, looking at Flynn and feeling all kinds of awful for having to be the one to drop this bomb. "They're only here because they needed your permit to access the reef…and they're trying to blow it up—with dynamite!—to get to some treasure they think is buried out here. Captain Jack put the dynamite down there on his dive earlier, and Lexi made me drop the timer when we went down together. It's ticking backward and it's set to blow up in a few hours!"

Captain Jack has his hands over his face. Lexi is full-on crying.

"They *were* trying to blow it up," Zac corrects me. "But Marina here overheard them talking about their plan. I didn't want to believe her at first. I really didn't. But I know she'd never lie to me, so I found my uncle's logbook. It's all in here, everything they were planning to do." He holds up the tattered book.

"Lexi, Jack, is this true? Please tell me it's not, please," Flynn pleads.

"It wasn't supposed to happen this way," Lexi cries. "We tried to get to the treasure without hurting anything. Really we did! And we were going to donate half of what we found to the Coral Reef Preservation Society. Weren't we, Jack? Tell them!"

"We did it for *you*, Zac," Captain Jack says, all choked up and red in the face. "That treasure is your legacy too, you know. It's your birthright. Your grandfather died because of it. With that money you could have saved hundreds of reefs! Yes, we were going to sacrifice one. But you can see the big picture here, can't you? Can't you?"

"And what was going to happen *after* you blew up that reef, Uncle Jack? Huh? We all would have had to escape in the dinghy. We'd be banned from the conservationist community forever, and we'd never have seen Flynn and Marina again! How could you do this to me when you know that nothing matters to me more than being an oceanographer someday? Not money, not some stupid buried treasure, nothing! My parents trusted you to take care of me, and you could have gotten me arrested or killed! And how could you do this to Flynn and Marina, after all they've done for us?" Zac wipes away a tear.

"We would have made it right," Lexi says. "You have to believe that, Zac!"

"Tell it to the judge," a guard says, slapping handcuffs on Captain Jack. Another guard locks up Lexi.

"I'm so, so sorry," Zac says, looking from me to Flynn and back again.

"I'm sorry too," I tell Zac.

"I'm in shock," Flynn says, shaking his head.

"Do I come with you?" Zac asks a guard in a tiny, sad voice.

"You stay here," a guard says, leading Captain Jack and the others onto the Coast Guard boat. "We'll need all of you to make statements of course, but there's time for that. Hey, both of you kids," he adds, nodding to me and Zac, "nice work here. You should feel very proud of yourselves."

Zac just hangs his head. I wrap my arms around him and squeeze him as tightly as I can.

"It's going to be okay, Zac," I tell him. "You did the right thing."

"Then why do I feel totally awful?" Zac asks.

For once in my life, I'm totally speechless.

Chapter 19

When I Don't Get to Say Good-bye

Once the Coast Guard boat leaves and is just a speck in the distance on the open sea, the *Sea Angel* is completely quiet. The sun looks like a big fireball hanging over the ocean, sending gorgeous purples, pinks, and oranges—my favorite color combo—across the sky against streams of lazy, puffy clouds. I can hear tiny waves lapping against the hull of the boat. It's so peaceful that it's hard to believe that this might have been the scene of an environmental disaster. And for what? Money? Don't get me wrong, I think the idea of a buried treasure is as cool as the next person—but not if you have to commit a crime to get it.

I walk out onto the deck where Zac is sitting by himself.

"I'm sorry about your aunt and uncle," I say because I have to say something.

"Yeah, it stinks when people turn out to not be what you think they are," Zac says.

"But it's better to know…right?" I say hopefully.

"I guess…" Zac trails off. "Want me to come with you on Skipper's evening swim?"

"Sounds great," I say with a smile, grabbing my goggles off a hook. I'm beyond exhausted, but I can tell Zac needs a friend right now—and I know he'd do it for me. He leans down and bangs the side of boat to call Skipper, who shows up squealing in about one second.

"Last one in is a steaming pile of…" I hear Zac say, but I've already taken a flying leap off the back of the boat.

"A steaming pile of what, Zac?" I ask, looking up from the water. Skipper nuzzles me under the arm as I tread water, laughing.

"A steaming pile of pancakes!" Zac yells, doing his best cannonball and spraying me with the big splash. This time I'm ready with a full breath when Skipper tucks his adorable nose under my arm and takes off.

We're flying through the water, and Zac is doing his perfect butterfly stroke behind. There's no way he can keep up with us.

Just like before, Skipper slows to a stop and motions with his whole head to the buoy in the distance. Zac catches up with us and we all race to the buoy. I do the breaststroke this time, and I'm wishing there was some way I could take these swimming skills back to the Mountain View Pool with me. I'd also like to take Zac and this precious dolphin, but I already know that's not how it works.

I get to the buoy before Zac, after Skipper of course, and give it a big slap before finding a place to hold on and catch my breath. Zac swims up next to me in a matter of seconds.

"I'm pretty sure you're part dolphin," he says between big breaths. "Which would explain your swimming *and* why Skipper has such a big crush on you."

Crush? Did he say crush? Oh wait, he was talking about Skipper. Still, it's too late to stop it. My face lights up like a traffic signal. I take a big breath and sink down into the water, floating like a big X. I'm only wearing a tiny pair of goggles and it's almost dark, but I can see a big sea turtle swimming by and bunches of beautiful fish flitting left and right. I can't believe I have to leave this underwater world behind. When I can't hold my breath any longer, I come back up for air and see Zac, holding on to the buoy and staring off toward the setting sun.

"It's still hard to believe my aunt and uncle are such horrible people," he says, shaking his head. "They've been like my parents out here all year long."

"Maybe they're not truly awful. Sometimes people forget what's important and do really bad things," I say, trying to come up with some helpful genie guidance on the fly, "because they want something so badly." I think about Brianna back at swim team tryouts. She wanted to be the best so badly that she was willing to do *anything* to get rid of a little competition.

"You're such a good friend, Marina," Zac says, looking straight at me. "And the only person in the world who could know exactly how I feel." I smile right back at him, once again at a loss for words.

Just then, Flynn rings the big, brass ship's bell to call us in for dinner. The same bell Captain Jack rang for lunch this afternoon. Could that really have been this afternoon? It feels like a million years ago.

Skipper circles back to us when he hears this, and the three of us swim back to the *Sea Angel*. I've never gotten to know anyone so well in one day in the MMBs. As I swim effortlessly back to the boat, I start to feel really sad that it's all going to be over soon. And I'll never see Zac or Skipper or Flynn again.

Flynn is waiting at the back of the boat with big beach towels for us. "You kids are heroes," he says, taking us under each arm. "I hope you realize that."

"Thanks Flynn," Zac says. He looks uncomfortable with the praise so I try to save him.

"More importantly, what's for dinner?" I ask.

"What else? Spaghetti and meatballs!" Flynn says with a smile. Sweeter words have never been spoken.

"Go get showered and meet me in the salon in fifteen, guys," Flynn tells us. I swing around the railing and go down the steep stairs. A shower sounds amazing right about now. After I get cleaned up, I slip into a striped cotton slip dress that's so soft it feels like it's been washed about seven dozen times and pull on a fleece hoodie. I pile my hair on top of my head the way Auntie Fi does. A few curls fall down, but honestly, I'm starving and can't be bothered by my misbehaving mane.

"Maybe the best spaghetti and meatballs I've ever had," I say, dotting my mouth with my napkin to make sure there's no tomato sauce smeared across my face as we finish eating. "Thank you, Flynn—I mean, Dad!" *Keep it together, Malone! You're in the last little stretch of this marathon day!*

Flynn just laughs. "You kids must be exhausted. I've got the dishes. You two go get some sleep," he says and kisses me on the forehead.

"See you in the morning, Marina," Zac says, looking back at me before he goes down the stairs.

"Okay...good night, Zac," I call back, because what else *can* I say? It's really hard not to say good-bye.

I sleepily brush my teeth with Marina's toothbrush. Kind of gross, I know, but think about it. Not a lot of options, right? I can't remember being this tired. Ever. I shuffle to the bed and literally fall into it. As the waves lap gently at the sides of the boat, I drift off into a deep, deep sleep.

Chapter 20

When I Have to Deal with What I Left Behind

"Way back when, before I knew, some fairy tales they just don't come true..."

Out of nowhere, my blissful sleep is interrupted by the sounds of Becca Starr's chart-topping hit. *Is this a sound check? Am I supposed to be on stage somewhere? Is the band rehearsing without me?* Wait a minute, I'm not Becca Starr anymore! I'm Marina Tide, ocean explorer, super swimmer, and most of all, friend to Skipper. And of course, Zac.

Zac.

I hit my snooze button and bolt upright in bed—a bed that's not rocking softly from side to side anymore—and pry my exhausted eyelids open. There's my cozy polka-dot chair in the corner. The purple vanity table that I helped my mom paint is right next to my closet, and my fluffy zebra-striped rug is right in the middle of it all. I'm home. I'm Maggie Malone again. And if I'm not mistaken or smack in the middle of some crazy dream, I saved an entire coral reef yesterday, swam with my own pet dolphin (well, he was my own for the day), dove clear down to the dark and faraway bottom of the ocean, and hung out with pretty much the coolest, sweetest (and cutest) guy on the planet.

The memories come flooding back, and I feel dizzier than the time Stella and I had a contest to see who could spin in a circle the most times in one minute. (I beat Stella sixty-three to sixty-one. And then I puked. But I won! I tried not to gloat or anything afterward though, because my dad always says if you're a poor winner, you might as well be the loser.)

I look at my wall calendar and realize it's Tuesday. The crazy thing about the MMBs—oh, who am I kidding? *Everything* about the MMBs is crazy! I guess maybe I should say *one* of the craziest things about the MMBs—is that time stops when I wear them. So even though I had this incredible, jam-packed day full of giant turtles and deep-sea diving and crime-busting and Zac, it was still only yesterday that I tried out for the swim team and made second alternate. Which means that my first practice, alongside Brianna, the pint-size witch of the Pinkerton Minnows, is today. And I was supposed to convince Elizabeth to quit… or else. Instead, she unfriended me because she thinks I'm a big, fat liar. *This* day ought to be fun.

After I get dressed and brush my teeth and scrunch my hair with wet hands, I stuff my goggles and new team suit into my backpack and breeze through the kitchen. I thought about just switching to yearbook, but then Elizabeth would be shark bait. Even though she doesn't want to be my friend anymore, I can't let her be munched by Brianna the piranha. There's a toasted bagel on the counter smeared with strawberry cream cheese, next to a note from my mom scrawled on a napkin in bright red Sharpie. "Hope you have the best day EVER. Love you more!"

That's kind of a thing we do. Whenever one of us says "love you," the other always says "love you more!" A lot of times my mom says just the "love you more" part, even though I didn't say anything first. When she does, it's like she's saying she already knows how much I love her, which makes me feel really good. I grab my bagel and run back toward her bathroom, where she's in the shower.

"Mom?" I shout through the bathroom door.

"What is it, sweetie?" she calls back.

"Love *you* the most!" I yell. "Bye!"

I take off, dashing out the front door and around to the side of the house where my bike is stashed. I jump on it and check my watch. Right on time to meet Stella! I can't wait to tell her everythi—

Rotten, stinking rats! Did I mention the other thing about the MMBs? Not a peep to anyone, not even Stella, or all of that magic will just disappear. How unfair is *that*? I mean, magic is cool and everything, but half of the fun of anything cool is sharing it with your BFF!

I coast to the corner of Spruce and Maple and wait for the light to change, my head swimming with a zillion thoughts. Poor Zac and how he must be feeling today on the boat. Elizabeth and how she thinks I'm a liar. Lexi and Captain Jack and the super-hot water they're in right this very minute. Tiny, two-faced Brianna and her giant threats. I shake my head to try to make those thoughts go away or at least settle them down a bit.

"Margaret Flannery Malone!" I hear from what feels like far, far away. "Earth to Maggie!" Stella is waving wildly at me from the opposite corner. I wave back and do the twirly-finger-to-the-temple move we always do when we bust each other daydreaming. The light changes and I pedal over to Stella's side.

"Well?" she demands right away. "How did tryouts go? I called you, like, eleventy billion times last night and emailed you at least fifteen more! The suspense is killing me!"

"Sorry," I tell her. "Tryouts were crazy and then I had this huge paper to write for English class, which by the way isn't nearly as fun as the English class at Sacred—"

Stella cuts me off. "*Did you make the team?*" she wants to know, rolling her eyes and doing the twirly-finger-to-temple move back at me.

"Oh, right, that!" I laugh. "Yeah, well, sort of. Second alternate. But it's better than nothing, right?"

"Way better," Stella agrees, giving me a thumbs-up while pedaling alongside me.

"Yeah, I guess…except there's this one thing," I tell Stella.

"What is it?" she wants to know. "And make it snappy, we've got to split up in two blocks!"

"Well, I tried out with my new friend Elizabeth from Pinkerton. I told you about her, right?" I say. "And it turns out she's, like, crazy good, which is great, but…"

"So? You're crazy good too!" Stella shouts, standing up on her bike pedals and doing a rolling dance in my honor.

"Thanks, Stella. She's, like, *Olympic* good, but that's not the problem. See, there's this kid on the team—she's actually the coach's daughter and her name's Brianna—and when Elizabeth kicked her butt in tryouts, Brianna told me that it was up to *me* to get Elizabeth to quit the team or she'd make both our lives miserable."

Stella actually laughs at this. "She's threatening *Margaret Flannery Malone*? She obviously doesn't know who she's dealing with! Does she know I taught you those super-fast and dangerous karate moves?" Stella thinks she's got skills like the star in *The Karate Girl*.

"The other problem," I tell Stella, looking at my watch, "is that I tried to tell Elizabeth what Brianna said…but she doesn't believe me. She thinks I'm making it all up because I'm jealous that she made the team and I'm only an alternate." My stomach sinks when I say this out loud.

"Well, then you just need to set her straight," Stella says. "If she's a real friend, she'll listen to you. Am I right? I mean, you either trust your friends or you don't. And if she's not smart enough to trust *you*, I say you're better off without her. Shoot, gotta run or I'll be late. You okay?" We're at the corner where we have to go in opposite directions.

"I'm good, Stella. Thanks," I tell her, trying to smile.

"Hey, Mags," she calls over her shoulder as she crosses the street. "You've got this."

That's what they all say, I think to myself as I cruise the last block to Pinkerton. I sure hope they're right.

Chapter 21

When It's Back to Being Invisible for Me

I see Elizabeth pulling up to the bike rack at the same time as me. I figure that's kind of perfect! We can get this misunderstanding straightened out before school starts. But a funny thing happens. Not funny like ha-ha; funny like a three-headed-monster coming after you—as in *not funny at all.*

"Hey, Elizabeth!" I say, locking up my bike. She parks hers on the opposite side of the rack.

I know she heard me, because she's *standing right there.* But she's pretending I didn't say a word, like somebody hit the Maggie Malone mute button or something.

"Elizabeth?" I say again as she pulls her book bag from the basket on her bike and slings it over her shoulder.

Nothing. She just looks straight ahead and walks away toward the multipurpose room.

Okey dokey. I get it. She's giving me the silent treatment. My mom always says if someone's not being nice, then you should just leave them alone and go find somebody else to hang out with. Since it's better than following Elizabeth around like a lost, pathetic puppy dog, I decide that's what I'll do.

I get to my locker, and wouldn't you know it? Clumsy Carl Lumberton is there, above my bottom locker. Papers and pencils and half-eaten stale sandwiches are pouring out of his locker like an avalanche.

"Organize much, Carl?" I say. He just looks at me with his mouth hanging half open and goes back to trying to get his locker shut. He's not much of a conversationalist.

I stand there for another three torturous minutes but it's no use. Carl might be here all day. I realize I have my Spanish notebook and textbook in my backpack so I decide to head straight to class.

"*Hola*, Margarita!" Señora Burro says when I walk in. Did you know that "burro" is Spanish for donkey? So back in her homeland, which I'm not sure but I think might be Mexico, they call her Mrs. Donkey. Maybe that's not considered a bad thing in Mexico, but around here, donkeys aren't known to the smartest ponies in the pasture, if you know what I mean.

I slide into a seat next to Alicia, who looks at me like two slimy tentacles just sprouted out of my head and are about to snatch her up and sling her to a pack of hungry wolves.

"Uh…oh, sorry, Maggie," Alicia says with a scared half-smile. "Winnie's sitting there."

"Wow, I didn't even see her," I say, pretending to look around. "I hope I didn't squish her too badly!" Alicia doesn't laugh.

"Well, she's not sitting there yet, but I'm saving it for her," Alicia says, not meeting my eyes.

She's saving a seat for Winnie Ipswitch? This is new.

"No prob," I say, plopping my book bag next to an empty seat behind Lucy.

"Actually, that one's for Elizabeth—she asked me to save it for her," Lucy says with a shrug.

"O…kay…" I mumble to myself. I can feel my face getting hot. I look around the room and finally find a seat against the cold cement wall at the way-back of the room.

I can't focus on gender-specific Spanish pronouns for one second, even though I know we're having a quiz tomorrow and this is probably my only shot at understanding them.

The truth of what's happening starts to sink in, and my eyes start filling up with tears. I swear my body has a mind of its own and is always insists on announcing to the world exactly how I'm feeling. Ugh. I try not to blink, but you know you can only do that so long. Finally when I do, a puddle of tears plops on the page where a guy is smiling and waving while riding a burro. This makes me laugh a little because I wonder if that donkey might be Mrs. Burro's second cousin.

I quickly swipe the tiny tear puddle off my page, and wouldn't you know it? It hits Carl Lumberton right in the arm. I figure he's going to look at me all mean like, *Thanks a lot for spitting on me, Malone*, but instead he looks down and wipes the corner of his mouth. He assumed he drooled on his own arm. I exhale a sigh of relief. You have to appreciate small victories at a time like this.

I lean back against the icy wall and wonder how everything got so bad so fast. So much for turning things around at Pinkerton.

Chapter 22

When Things Get Worse at the Mountain View Pool

Every other class is pretty much a repeat of Spanish class—socially speaking, anyway. The only break I get all day is during speech class, because it's the one class I don't share with any of my "friends." When lunchtime finally arrives, I snatch my lunch bag from my locker and race over to the auditorium. I go to the back where all the costumes are hanging behind the red velvet curtain and climb between racks of smelly clothes and pull out my genie pocket mirror.

"Frank! Oh, Frank, best genie in the whole wide world!" I sing, hoping that a little appreciation might encourage him to show up faster and, I don't know, maybe stick around long enough so I can give him the full lowdown.

"Mags!" he says, his face coming into focus. "You're already back at school. Hey, nice work out there on the ocean! That's what I'm talking about. You figured it out and all on your own, Magpie—I told you that you could!"

"Oh that, yeah…thanks, Frank!" I say, smiling, because it *was* all kinds of awesome out there.

I was calling Frank for some genie advice on how to deal with these girls being so mean to me, but he gives me an idea.

"Hey, speaking of that, Frank," I say in a nice, but hopefully not over-the-top sweet voice. "I'd like to take another spin as Marina Tide. Like right now, please. And thank you."

Why not? I was super helpful on the *Sea Angel* and jumping back into her life would be a quick escape out of my own life, which as of eight o'clock this morning has become the exact opposite of *all kinds of awesome.*

"Oh Maggie, darlin', you know that's not how it works," Frank says, shaking his head. "You only get one day in somebody else's life. That's why I always say you'd better make it good!"

"Okay. I know, then I'll be somebody else

lickety-split, Frank. Got any good ideas for me? I just have to run home and get the MMBs and—"

"Hold on there, cowgirl. You know the MMBs aren't about stepping into somebody else's life when things in your own life get tough," Frank says, looking straight at me. I have to tell you, but when a genie looks you straight in the eyeballs, it's about impossible to look away. I see a colorful boat float by behind Frank and realize he's on a river somewhere.

"Where in the world are you, Frank?" I ask, because he is one globe-trotting genie.

"Early morning on the Ganges, Mags! India. You do *not* want to know what's in that water," he says, motioning over his shoulder at the murky water behind him.

"Ewww," I agree, taking his word for it. "I guess I don't."

"You just saved a fragile, endangered coral reef, my dear," Frank says and I can tell he's about to sign off.

"Wait, Frank!" I plead, falling against Mr. Mooney's crown and scepter.

"Now go *save yourself*!" he calls out just as his image turns back to my own.

Save myself? Genies!

At the end of the longest, loneliest school day of my life, I race cheetah-like to my locker and grab all of my gear. I'm hoping to make it to the bike rack quickly so that I can catch Elizabeth before she takes off for practice at Mountain View Pool. I know she's technically not speaking to me, but I'm determined to turn that around. Even though I booked it, when I get to the rack her turquoise ten-speed is already gone. I huff the six blocks to the pool feeling about as lonely as a stowaway mouse on a ship at sea.

I check in at the front desk and get a locker key. That makes me feel better for a split second. I don't know why, but I love having my own locker key. My miniature bubble bursts before I even get to the locker-room door. How am I going to get Elizabeth to forgive me when she won't even *talk* to me? She has to come around sooner or later, doesn't she? I just wish I knew how to make it sooner. The whole point of this stupid swim team was to do it together, to be a part of something. And right now, the only thing I'm part of is a big, fat nothing.

I take a deep breath and push open the locker-room

door. Most of the swim team is in there getting ready, and every head in the room swings to look at me. Nobody says a word. "Hi guys!" I say as brightly as I can. My words echo off the tile walls. If my life were a movie, they'd be playing a sound track of crickets right now.

"Want to do a few warm-up laps before practice starts?" Brianna asks Elizabeth, totally ignoring me and linking her arm through my friend's. Elizabeth gives me the Look ("Oh yeah, Maggie, she's really making my life *miserable* here.") before turning to parade out the side door to the pool, arm-in-arm with the Mountain View Monster.

I wait until everyone else shuffles out, and then I tuck into a bathroom stall and try not to cry. *Get it together, Malone. You can fix this. You can! You stopped a pair of cold, hard criminals from destroying something endangered and beautiful yesterday! And you convinced everyone on that boat that people they thought they could trust were rotten to the core. Of course, you had Zac's help with that one. Who can help you now? Think. THINK!*

"MALONE, ARE YOU IN HERE?" A male voice booms through the locker room.

"Coming, Coach!" I shout back, hoping he's not actually *in the room* looking for me.

"Well, hurry it up. I'm waiting right outside and I need to talk to you," he barks.

I quickly splash some water on my face, grab my towel and goggles, and head toward the huge glass door that leads to Mountain View's famous pool. When I swing the door open, Coach King is waiting outside it, just like he promised. "Brianna says you didn't want to do your practice laps today," he says before I can even get a word out.

"Well, actually, sir, that's not exactly—"

Coach King cuts me off.

"Listen, Malone, you're part of this team, and like it or not, I'm the boss of this team. I made it pretty clear that you had some work to do, and Brianna was nice enough to offer to help you. Turn her down again and I'll have to seriously consider removing you for good." He turns and strides off toward the pool, where the rest of the team is waiting.

"But Coach—" I say, following him. My voice echoes through the gigantic tiled room. "That's not—"

Brianna has picked up on what's happening and she jumps right in.

"It's okay, Maggie," she says in a sickeningly sweet voice. "We can work on your strokes tomorrow if you want. I'd be *more* than happy to do that for you. Even though, you know, today..."

"But you never offered to swim with me today!" I wail. "You didn't. In fact, you didn't even say *hello* to me." I'm making a bit of a scene here, but I am downright furious.

She's lying through her teeth!

"I did too," Brianna shrieks, even louder than me. "Didn't I, Elizabeth? Didn't I offer to help Maggie today, and didn't she say *no* right to my face? And wasn't she totally rude about it on top of it all?"

Everyone looks at Elizabeth. *Come on, friend. Don't throw me under the bus! You were right there, and you know for a fact that she's totally lying. Do the right thing, pretty-please-with-sugar-on-top.*

Elizabeth opens her mouth to say something, then closes it. Instead, she nods her head just the tiniest bit.

I'm not sure, but I think the tiny gasp that comes out of my own mouth is the sound of my heart ripping in half.

Chapter 23

When I Save Myself

Every day at school for the rest of the week is pretty much a repeat of my terrible Tuesday. It doesn't take a super sleuth to figure out that Elizabeth went around and told all of our friends that I'm a lying, conniving sack of sour snails and so nobody—I mean, nobody—wants to have anything to do with me. Here's what I don't get: Why was Elizabeth so quick to believe the worst? And also, why was everybody else so willing to join forces with her?

My mom says this sort of thing is just part of middle school. That's pretty depressing considering I'm in the sixth grade and have two more years of this. Frank says it's up to me to save myself. I'm starting to think that's his genie stock answer for everything, but in this case, I'm pretty sure he's right. I mean, I don't see anybody else stepping up to the plate to swing for me.

I just deal with Wednesday and Thursday and look forward to Friday afternoon when I can hang out with Stella and we can ride our bikes to Dippin' Donuts and eat double-dunked chocolate doughnuts as big as flying saucers. But when Friday finally rolls around, I remember I have swim team practice. *Ugh!* I huff it up the hill to the Mountain View Pool, walk into the locker room, and pull out my swimsuit. If I could set this ugly one-piece on fire, I would. But obviously I can't do that. I have to come up with another plan, and so far I've got nothing. So I'm sitting on the toilet. More like crouching on top of the seat so no one can see me.

Someone walks into the bathroom. I peek through the crack between the stall and the door and see that it's Brianna. Luckily she can't see me. She's swinging a pair of goggles around her index finger and talking in a voice that sounds an awful lot like one of those evil queens in a Disney movie.

"Let's see how well you swim the fifty-yard freestyle

without your goggles, Elizabeth O'Connor," she says into the mirror and then breaks into a devilish laugh as she shoves the goggles to the bottom of the towel bin. Once she's satisfied that the goggles will never be found, Brianna turns, clasps her tiny hands behind her back, and whistles as she leaves the bathroom. I slide off the pot, sneak out of the stall, and fish out Elizabeth's goggles. I wrap them in my towel and head for the door.

Coach blows his whistle just as I hit the deck. "Okay, we've got to get you guys ranked today for the meet," he says. "Brianna, Elizabeth, Ellie, and Amanda, on your blocks."

Everyone goes over to their hook, takes their goggles, and pulls them down across their eyes. Everyone except Elizabeth. I'm not sure how to break the news that I've got them.

"Coach?" Elizabeth says, confused. "My goggles are gone. I put them on the hook and now they're gone."

"Well, Elizabeth, if you put them on the hook, don't you think they'd still be on the hook?" Coach asks, squinting his eyes.

"I *know* they were there, Coach. I—" Elizabeth starts, but Coach interrupts her.

"Go home and read your rule book, Elizabeth," he says sharply. "You either show up with all of your gear, ready to practice, or you sit out the next meet. Jennifer, you're up!"

"But I promise, I…" Elizabeth says and looks like she's definitely going to cry.

"Save it!" Coach says, holding up his huge hand like a stop sign.

"Wait, aren't these your goggles, Elizabeth?" I call out, holding hers up.

"Yes! Yes, they are!" Elizabeth cries. She rushes over to me, looking relieved and also more than a little bit confused.

Brianna narrows her eyes at me. "Wait," she screams. "Those aren't Elizabeth's goggles! Maggie is just trying to cover for her!"

"Actually Brianna, these *are* my goggles," Elizabeth says, holding them up for Brianna to see. "See, *EO*? My initials. My mom makes me put them on everything. But how did *you* get them, Maggie?"

Every eye on that pool deck is on me and I can feel my face turning purple.

"I found them in the locker room," I say.

"She's lying, Dad!" Brianna yells. "She took them!"

"Really?" Coach asks. "Why would the second alternate bother to steal anybody's goggles? And more importantly, why would she give them back?" He sounds more than a little impatient.

"I don't know," Brianna says, pouting. "But I know she took them." She points at me when she says this.

"Well, it looks like you know wrong and you're wasting everyone's time here," he says, turning away dismissively. "As I was saying, swimmers, on your marks!"

Brianna gives me a seriously scary stink eye. I pretend not to see her.

"Tell me the truth, Maggie," Elizabeth says after practice as we're packing up our stuff. "How did you get my goggles?"

"You think I took them, don't you?" I ask Elizabeth, my heart sinking. I can hear Stella's words ringing in my ears: *If she's not smart enough to trust you, you're better off without her.*

"No, actually I *know* you wouldn't do that," Elizabeth says. "But I also know that I put them on my hook. So something's up. Just tell me."

"Brianna took them and hid them in the towel bin," I tell her. "I was in the bathroom stall and I saw her do it."

"I had a feeling she had something to do with it," Elizabeth says, shaking her head. "But why didn't you call her out? She'd have been automatically disqualified for that!"

I shrug. "I guess I was getting tired of people not believing me," I tell her. "Besides, won't it be way more fun to beat her fair and square?"

Elizabeth nods and smiles at me, and I want to explode with happiness. She forgives me! We're friends again! I can't wait to tell Frank that I actually did it. I saved myself by being myself.

Chapter 24

When the Whole Truth Comes Out

"I'm a horrible, smelly turd," Elizabeth says as we're unlocking our bikes. "I feel awful for not believing you about Brianna. And even worse than awful that I didn't stand up for you when she lied about the practice laps. And not just because you saved my butt, but also because you're a great friend. I told everyone you were a liar and you didn't deserve that. *I'm* the liar."

Elizabeth looks as miserable as I feel.

"Well, actually," I say, pretending to be very busy working my bike lock. "I might not have been *totally* honest..."

"What do you mean?" Elizabeth asks.

"I pinkie-promise you that Brianna said she was going

to make your life miserable," I say, crossing my heart and holding up my pinkie when I do. "Mine too. She even poked me in the chest really hard when she said it."

"Okay, then… What is it?" Elizabeth wants to know.

"I might have made up the head shaving and Ex-Lax stories," I say, nearly tripping over my words. "But I was desperate! I needed you to believe me, and I couldn't think of any other way to get you to quit the team. I'm sorry I lied to you. I feel awful."

Elizabeth looks at me for what feels like a million years. I'm actually holding my breath.

"Well, you wouldn't have had to if I had listened to you in the first place," she finally says, and I want to cry happy tears. "I should have known better. I just got so crazy about making the team that I wanted to believe you were a liar so I didn't have to quit. I guess I never really thought I could measure up to my dad and my brother, and when I found out I might actually be good at swimming, I started to want it so badly that I couldn't think straight."

"I get that," I tell her. "So, are we friends again?"

"Do you really want to be friends with somebody who told everyone you're a big, fat liar?" Elizabeth asks, looking at the ground. "That was an awful thing to do. I'll do anything to make it up to you." She looks like she's about to lose it, and since I know exactly how she feels, I want to cheer her up.

"Would you clean out Carl Lumberton's smelly locker?" I ask.

"Yes!" she says, laughing.

"Would you wear your hair in seven braids for seven days?" I ask her.

"Yes! Anything!" Elizabeth says. "That would *not* be a good look for me, but yes, if you'll forgive me for being such a humongous jerk, I'll tie rainbow-colored ribbons on the end of every braid!"

"Okay," I say, slinging my leg over my bike and hopping on. "Maybe you could just tell Alicia and Winnie and Lucy that I'm *not* a big, fat liar."

"Done," Elizabeth says, giving me a sheepish smile. "And Maggie, I *am* really, really—"

"I know," I tell her, hooking my helmet. "Me too. It's all good. Race you to the light!" I take off before she can even answer me, which isn't exactly fair, but since she just crushed me like a bug in the pool, I figure she'll let me have this. And she does. We're both laughing and panting when we reach the light.

"Thanks for being so...so Maggie," she calls over her shoulder as we break to go to our separate houses.

For some reason, as I'm riding home, I think about the letter Auntie Fi sent with the MMBs. "You get to decide how big you want your life to be," it said. I guess if we all started scratching people off our friend list because they made a mistake, our lives would get pretty small pretty fast. I'm really glad that didn't happen. I think Auntie Fi would be proud of us, and this makes me smile as I'm rounding the corner into my driveway.

Alicia calls me that night to apologize, which feels really good. "I should have known that you'd never try to hurt Elizabeth—or any of us," she says, and that makes me feel even better. "And you know what Monday is, right?" she adds. "The big pep rally to kick off Spirit Week! You and Elizabeth get to sit with the swim team. Sweeeeeet!"

I'd forgotten about the pep rally. Normally the weekends fly by and all of a sudden it's Monday morning again and I'm not even sure where the time went, but this weekend seems to drag on and on. Funny how that happens when you're excited about something.

When Monday morning finally rolls around, I put on cute jean shorts and the "Just Keep Swimming" T-shirt my mom bought me when I made the team (I'm assuming we don't wear our swimsuits under our cover-ups, right?), and then I tie my Pinkerton Minnows bathrobe over it. It isn't *technically* a bathrobe, but that's pretty much what it looks like. I feel a little silly riding my bike in this getup at first with my terry-cloth belt flapping in the breeze—especially when Stella sees me and shouts, "Hey Maggie, you forgot to get dressed!"—but after we pass a girl in a feather cap and a boy in a suit and *bow tie*, I realize it really doesn't matter. Besides, I would put on an alien costume with tentacles sticking out of the ears if it meant I didn't have to sit in Siberia with Mrs. Shankshaw and Mrs. Grossbottom at the pep rally.

I cruise up to Pinkerton and Elizabeth is by the bike rack waiting for me.

"I brought you something," she says shyly, pulling a Dippin' Donuts bag out of her backpack.

"Wow, thanks!" I tell her, sliding a giant, sticky glazed doughnut from the bag. "You must have gotten up early today to get this."

"That's what friends are for, right?" She smiles and we head to the Pit Bull Arena together. Mr. Mooney is waiting outside, and he's dressed up—wait for it— like a giant pit bull. He's wearing a full-body suit that looks like it's made out of brown shag carpet, with paws for his hands and feet and everything.

"May I please have your attention?" he calls out, and when he does, he reaches back and flips the car- peted suit's hoodie up onto his head. It's got two little pointy ears sticking straight up on top. He totally looks like a pit bull! Just when I think this can't pos- sibly get any better, he turns around so that his back is facing everyone and shakes his stubby little tail, just like a puppy would. The crowd goes wild.

"You've got to give it to him," I tell Elizabeth with a laugh. "The guy's got school spirit!"

"He's not the only one," says Alicia, sliding into place next to me. She's wearing her soccer uniform, of course, and she has the words "pit" and "bulls" painted in bright red lipstick on her cheeks.

She pulls two neon-pink swim caps out of her bag and hands one to me and the other to Elizabeth. She'd written "Don't Mess with the Minnows" on the sides of each.

"I'm game if you are," I tell Elizabeth, tugging that thing down onto my head. I didn't squish my crazy curls up into it first, so I'm sure I look like that clown in the bald-head cap who came to Stella's eighth birthday party and couldn't even make a decent balloon wiener dog, but do you know what? I honestly don't care. Elizabeth pulls her cap on too. Her straight blond hair sticks tightly to her neck, and her round face looks even rounder.

"Am I cute?" she asks with a laugh.

"Adorable," I insist. Because she is.

Chapter 25

When I Have to Bite My Tongue. Again.

When I get home from school, Stella is sitting on my front porch.

"I couldn't find the hide-a-key!" she says, standing up. "Did your mom hide it from me again?"

"Well, you *do* keep taking the keys home in your pocket..." I say, one eyebrow raised, while unlocking the door.

"Oh yeah, there is that." Stella chuckles. "I could make a pretty good wind chime with that pile of Malone hide-a-keys I have at my house!"

Stella called last night to see if I could help her with her math this afternoon, because, well, I am pretty good at math and her new math teacher at Sacred Heart teaches class using Marty the Math Wiz MeTube videos. I can tell you for sure that once the higher-ups at Sacred Heart catch wind of that, she'll be tossed out like last week's lasagna.

We fix a fancy afternoon snack of cheese and crackers on a tray with a side of purple grapes—*ooh-la-la!*—and use the tall, blue plastic wineglasses for our milk.

"Oh Mags!" Stella says, plopping down on my bed and chomping on a cracker. "Did you hear about the huge scandal on Marina Tide's boat last week?"

I'm distracted by the cracker crumbs falling from Stella's mouth and collecting on my comforter. I really love Stella, but she eats a cracker like the Cookie Monster eats a cookie, and I can already feel those crumbs on the back of my legs when I get into bed tonight. Wait, did she say scandal? Marina Tide?

"No!" I lie, brushing the crumbs off my bed. "What happened?"

"Well, hand me your computer," Stella says, wiping her face with the back of her hand. "I saw it on the Daily Scoop."

As she's pulling up the web page, Stella summarizes the story for me. "So basically, Marina and her dad are in big trouble 'cause they were planning to blow up this coral reef to get some buried treasure and…"

"No, that's not how it—" I stop myself. "I mean, are you sure that's what happened? They're conservationists…maybe it was somebody else, like somebody on their boat and not Marina and her dad?"

"Maybe…" Stella says scrolling down the web page, looking for the story. "All I know is, I saw *Sea Goddess*—that's the name of her boat—and 'plan to destroy coral reef' and 'buried treasure.' I think that pretty much says it all, don't you think?"

First of all, it's the Sea ANGEL! I want to say, but I don't. I can't.

"There it is," I say, pointing to a headline. Stella clicks on the link and I scan the story quickly, relieved to see that they got the facts straight.

"It wasn't Marina and her dad," I say, pointing to the mug shots of Lexi and Captain Jack looking not at all happy. "These are the guys who were planning to blow up the reef to find the treasure."

I scroll down some more and see a picture of Zac

standing with Flynn's arm around his shoulders. Stella perks up.

"Mother of a mongoose! Who's the hottie?" Stella clicks on the picture to zoom in.

Can I tell you I am dying—*dying!*—to tell her that the hottie's name is Zac, and as cute as he looks on the computer screen, he's about a billion times cuter in person—not to mention funny and sweet. And then I think about when he held both of my hands and looked me in the eyes, and I thought I'd melt on the spot and how I never got to say good-bye.

"Earth to Maggie!" Stella says, waving her hands in front of my face. "Come in, Maggie!"

I shake my head a little to focus.

"Seriously, dude. Where do you *go* when you check out like that?" Stella asks. "You might want to talk to Dr. Stapleton about that, because my uncle Vern? He started staring off into space, and next thing we knew, he got caught streaking down the cereal aisle at the Shop 'n Save. True story."

"Okay, first of all, eww!" I tell Stella. "I really, *really* wish I didn't just see your uncle Vern naked in my brain. And second of all, I hardly think that a little daydreaming is reason to enough to go sit in that smelly, vomit-covered waiting room at the pediatrician's office."

"Yeah, I think you're fine," Stella agrees.

I sit back on my bed and pull Stella's heavy backpack into my lap.

"What do you have in here, Willis Freedman?" I laugh, pulling out her math book.

"Very funny!" Stella scowls. "I'm so done with him," she insists.

"Uh-huh," I agree, even though I don't believe it for a second. Because while there are some things you absolutely *have* to deal with, there are other things that are best left alone.

Maggie Malone's
Totally Fab Vocab

Just like I love to try out new lives, I also love to try out new words! Here's a list of some sort-of-fancy words I used in this book that you might not have known before. I included a synonym for each, but you could probably figure out what they mean from the way I used them in the story. Now that you know these words, don't be afraid to use them. Being smart is totally cool.

1. Abandon: to leave
2. Alternate: substitute
3. Anchovies: small saltwater fish
4. Antsy: overly excited
5. Apparently: clearly
6. Avalanche: large mass falling suddenly
7. Bellows: roars

8. Blares: makes loud noise
9. Bow: front of a boat
10. Buoy: a floating marker
11. Capacity: ability
12. Civilized: polite
13. Commotion: disturbance
14. Complexion: skin tone
15. Concussion: brain injury due to a blow to the head
16. Conservation: the act of preserving or protecting
17. Conversationalist: a person skilled at speaking with another person
18. Depressing: really sad
19. Desperate: extreme
20. Dilemma: problem
21. Dillydallying: wasting time
22. Dismissively: indicating lack of interest
23. Distracted: preoccupied
24. Earshot: within range to be heard
25. Effortlessly: easily
26. Embroidery: weaving with thread
27. Endangered: in danger of becoming extinct
28. Exertion: physical effort

29. Exotic: unusual
30. Expression: a particular phrase
31. Extracurricular: additional
32. Fiasco: disaster
33. Flitting: fluttering
34. Fuming: feeling or showing anger
35. Furious: extremely angry
36. Ganges: a sacred river in India
37. Gestures: hand movements
38. Glide: slide
39. Hauls: pulls
40. Humongous: huge
41. Hygiene: cleanliness
42. Jostle: bump and shake
43. Legitimate: official
44. Maintenance: upkeep
45. Milling: walking
46. Miniature: tiny
47. Minnow: small freshwater fish
48. Oceanographer: a scientist who studies the ocean
49. Officially: formally
50. Pathetic: pitiful
51. Plunge: to jump or dive into water

52. Privilege: honor

53. Professional: expert

54. Reflection: mirror image

55. Rhythm: particular beat

56. Scandal: disgraceful action

57. Scrawled: written sloppily

58. Sprawling: spreading out

59. Sprouted: suddenly appeared

60. Stash: tuck away for safekeeping

61. Stateroom: a bedroom on a ship

62. Stern: back of a boat

63. Summarizes: recaps

64. Synchronized: exactly together

65. Technically: officially

66. Throng: crowd

67. Thunderous: loud

68. Timidly: shyly

69. Torturous: painful

70. Trawler: large boat

71. Wedging: squeezing

About the Authors

Jenna McCarthy is a writer, speaker, and aspiring drummer who has wanted magical boots since she learned to walk. She lives with her husband, daughters, cats, and dogs in sunny Southern California.

Carolyn Evans is an author, speaker, and singer/songwriter who once opened for Pat Benatar—you can ask your mom who that is. She loves traveling to faraway places but is just as happy at home with her husband and kids, living by a river in South Carolina and dreaming up grand adventures for Maggie Malone.

MAGGIE MALONE AND THE MOSTLY MAGICAL BOOTS

Jenna McCarthy and Carolyn Evans

FOR MAGGIE MALONE, EVERY DAY IS FREAKY FRIDAY WITH THE HELP OF HER VERY SPECIAL NEW BOOTS.

When Maggie Malone's Aunt Fi gives her a pair of used, scuffed, plain brown boots for her birthday, she's less than impressed. Why couldn't her life be more like tween-pop sensation Becca Star? Instead, Maggie's stuck going to a new school in ugly boots. Until she wakes up in Becca's shoes—literally. Maggie's new boots are magical. They won't make broccoli taste like macaroni and cheese, but they will let her spend a day in the life of anyone she chooses.

MAGGIE MALONE GETS THE ROYAL TREATMENT

Jenna McCarthy and Carolyn Evans

WALKING A MILE IN SOMEONE ELSE'S SHOES CAN BE A ROYAL PAIN.

Every day is Freaky Friday for Maggie Malone and her Mostly Magical Boots. Whenever she slips on the MMBs, Maggie gets to be whomever she wants for a whole day. And whose life could be more fun to try on than the glamorous Princess Wilhelmina of Wincastle's? Even better, Wilhelmina is a bridesmaid in the Royal Wedding of the Century!

But even pampered princesses have whopper-sized problems—and hers is an evil archenemy named Penelope. Will she survive Penelope's tricks or will the whole wedding turn into a royal disaster?